M19:
The Beginning
ADAM ROOD

Published in the UK in 2021 by Proud to be Me

Paperback ISBN 978-1-9993784-0-0
eBook   ISBN 978-1-9993784-1-7

Illustrations by Lesley Danson and Lorraine Wilkins

Cover design and typeset by SpiffingCovers

M19:
The Beginning
ADAM ROOD

BOOK ONE OF THE EPIC M19 ADVENTURE SERIES

★ ★ ✦ ★ ✦

For my Dad, who would be so proud
to see this book published.

ONE

Billy stopped writing. He looked around at his classmates scratching pens on their paper, frantically finishing their sentences. Mrs Clinch was walking around. He could tell she was near him as the air stank of cabbage. With less than thirty seconds ticking on the clock, he looked down at his scrambled answers on the page and took a deep breath.

He was good at maths. He had received good marks in his English tests and his science knowledge was improving all the time. This test was different. All of these weird questions where there appeared to be no right or wrong answers.

He stared down at the final question and the short answer he'd given. Other people seemed to have written really long paragraphs and he'd just written six words. How difficult could it be to answer such a simple question he was thinking? He read it again just to check he'd understood.

'If you had one superpower, what would it be?'

Billy looked over at Mrs Clinch who was staring at the second hand of the clock so intently that she poured half of her coffee over her chin when she lifted it up to her face. It was like watching a vampire addicted to caffeine. She dabbed her chin with her floral blouse and looked around to see if anyone had noticed. Billy moved his head quickly to pretend that he hadn't seen. Coffee, he thought, is bound to smell better than cabbages.

'Stop writing please,' Mrs Clinch squealed. The sound echoed around the room. Thankfully Billy was sat the right way round. As his left ear didn't work as well as the right, he always tried to position himself so that his left side was nearest to her so that her shrill shriek didn't make him wince. He remembered his Dad saying after parents' evening, 'She's clearly a good teacher, but I swear her voice could pierce skin.' Billy told Dad about repositioning himself in class to his advantage and Dad joked, 'Good move son. Do you want me to block the other ear as well?'

Mrs Clinch began moving around the tables, collecting up the papers one by one. When she had eventually finished, she let out a sigh like she'd just run a marathon. 'That,' she said, 'is an hour of your lives that you'll never get back. I apologise on behalf of the Department of Education.'

She then went on to waste a full fifteen minutes ranting about government ministers and stupid tests. Nobody understood what she was going on about. The boredom was broken when Danny Thompson yawned loudly. As he threw his head backwards, open-mouthed, he fell off his chair.

All of a sudden, the smell of cabbage intensified as Mrs Clinch rushed over, like a scene from a television hospital drama. She shouted for Ruby to run and get the school nurse, despite Danny standing up almost straight away and giggling to himself.

It was unusual for people to talk about work during the lunch break, but this particular test had been so odd that nobody could help it. Even the demon dinner lady knew about it. She was the grumpiest, least hygienic dinner lady in the

world, often wiping her nose on her apron before spooning the beef stew into your bowl. Billy found her quite funny. She was one of those people who spoke incredibly loudly at him. He often met them: old people in the supermarket; aunty Rita; uncle Dave; and, Mrs Somerset from next door. Dad and Billy had nicknamed them 'the loudspeakers.' The Demon Dinner Lady was one of them.

'HOW. WAS. THE. TEST. DEAR?' she shouted in Billy's face. Just for fun, everyday Billy would shout back at her with pauses after every word too. 'QUITE. BORING.' he replied, loudly.

By the end of the day, Mrs Clinch was practically in tears with all of her pent-up test frustration from the morning and as it turned five minutes past three, Billy was delighted to be leaving.

He grabbed his backpack from the peg and began the short walk home, to find his mother stood in the kitchen.

'Hello darling. How was the test?'

Billy looked at her, surprised. This test had been a shock to everybody that morning.

'How did you know?' he said inquisitively. 'It's been all over the news,' she said 'they haven't stopped talking about it all day. Top secret reasons. Sudden tests. The whole country really cross. People refused to do it in some schools in London and went outside the Houses of Parliament to protest.'

'It was fine, Mum. Just, some odd questions...'

'Like what?'

'Like...' Billy paused for a moment. Maybe the government didn't really want adults to know. The questions were super weird and perhaps they were keeping a close eye on those parents who complained and would set off a million stink bombs at the houses of those who dared to moan about it.

'Just weird stuff, that's all...' he said. Then, Billy did something that he never did. Hesitantly, he looked up at his Mum, took a deep breath and said, 'How was your day?'

Mum smiled and then her cheeks started flushing the way they did when Billy gave her the locket that Dad had bought on behalf of him for her birthday, or the times when Dad would say 'I love you Sandy' and kiss her cheek on a Sunday afternoon. It made Billy feel sick.

'You're such a sweet boy. Thank you for asking. I took your Nan out for some lunch, did some paperwork and then made a start on this washing up.' she said smiling.

'That sounds like the most boring day ever.' Billy replied, kicking off his school shoes and casting his bag aside like finishing the end of an apple.

'You can help with the drying up if you like?'

Billy was already halfway up the stairs and pretended he couldn't hear, a trick that worked with some people - but not with Mum. She knew. Five minutes later he was stood, tea towel in hand, wishing for the end of the world to come before he had to dry any more plates. Mum was singing quietly. Billy always thought her singing voice sounded like a cross between a strangled cat and a dying frog but could never place it exactly. The previous year at Christmas, Billy and Dad had to go and watch her singing carols with the local choir. It was set to be the most boring evening of his life, until the local vicar choked on a mince pie and had to be given mouth to mouth resuscitation halfway through 'Silent Night.' When the lyrics got to 'All is calm' a large piece of pastry shot out of Father Derick's mouth and straight into the eye of Aileen Hesketh-Smythe, who was playing the organ.

By the time Dad got home from work, Billy had listened to three news bulletins about the morning's test. The protests had grown in numbers and it looked like half of London was ready to storm into the Houses of Parliament, screaming and shouting.

Nobody seemed to quite get to the bottom of what was actually on the test itself. Children were interviewed and had admitted to taking the test but couldn't really remember many of the questions. They had a vague idea and could remember sitting there, but not about what had been asked of them.

At dinner, Dad was joking over his plate of chilli con carne that perhaps everyone who had taken it had been poisoned, or perhaps every teacher was in on it and had zapped all of their pupils with a Dr-Who-style pen. All of a sudden, Billy's heart began beating really fast and he was swirling rice around his plate, desperate to leave the table so he could think.

'Can I go to bed? I'm really tired.' Billy said. Mum looked at Dad carefully. 'Absolutely,' she said, 'but if you think you're going to get away with sitting on that X-machine-thing all night, I'm afraid you're mistaken.' Billy had no intention of playing computer games, he, for the first time in his life was trying to search for clues with the mystical bottle of water.

TWO

Billy lay in bed, running through all of the events for a third time. Mrs Clinch had placed a copy of the test face down in front of each person. She then went back to her desk, opened the plastic top of a large box full of bottles of water and put one in front of everybody.

This was strange. Anybody could drink water whenever they wanted to at school. It wasn't uncommon, particularly on hot days, to see water bottles at every table in lessons after lunch. People would swig from water bottles that they had brought in from home all afternoon and if you got particularly desperate, you could visit the water fountain.

Before the test began, Mrs Clinch opened a sealed envelope and read an instruction sheet. She said something about it being important to be well hydrated before starting on the questions, so 'feel free to sip the water provided whenever you wish.'

Almost everyone unscrewed the cap of their water bottle and began glugging. Billy didn't.

He thought back and could distinctly remember thinking that it just looked like any other bottle of water. He tried to study the label in his mind, what it looked like, the colours and shapes...but he just couldn't recall it.

Billy sat up sharply. It was pitch black. He had fallen asleep, he still had his school uniform on, and Mum had clearly popped in and turned his light out when she had gone to bed. He looked across at his clock and it read '3:06 AM'

He had that horrible feeling that you get when you fall asleep fully clothed, like sleeping on a train or an aeroplane. His skin was clammy, and he had absolutely no desire to undress and put his pyjamas on.

But he was desperate for the toilet. A few moments before his bladder actually exploded, he stood up and walked across his bedroom floor. He knew that turning his light on would make him feel even more disgusting, so he chose to find his way to the toilet in the dark.

Bad move. Mum had also brought his school bag and PE kit up to his room and left it by the door. His foot got caught in the strap and he fell forwards flat onto his face. After scrambling back from the toilet, not wanting to make the same mistake a second time, he picked his school bag up and threw it across the room.

Soon afterwards, he heard a thump on the floor. As loud noises were often a little quieter to him, he was worried at first that it would've woken Mum and Dad. Billy, being so intrigued, had to switch the light on to see what it was. After his eyes had grown accustomed to the light and he was squinting a little less, he found the thump culprit. There, on the floor, was the bottle of water he'd been trying to picture. He remembered putting it in his bag at the end of the test. He picked it up and studied it closely.

The front of the bottle simply read 'mineral water' in a similar font to what you'd see on any bottled water in a supermarket. The back of the bottle was blue and green, with the government 'Department of Education' logo clearly visible across the middle. Nothing extraordinary at all. He sat there thinking and as he did so, his finger was peeling away at the label join on the bottle.

There was something written in tiny writing, beneath the top flap of plastic label. 'Ingredients: Pure Mineral Water bottled from Scottish Highlands. EMC249.'

Nothing funny about that, he thought. In the comfort of his pyjamas, sliding between the warmth of his bedsheets, he reached out for the bottle and unscrewed the cap. He took a large swig of water, placed the bottle back down and went to sleep.

THREE

Billy was walking down a murky corridor. It smelt of dust and damp and it was decorated like something out of an old book. The wallpaper was pink and yellow and there were pictures of important looking people on the wall, wearing medals and holding swords.

The lady in front of him was dressed like a headteacher. Her hair was scraped back, and her jacket flailed out to the side as she moved. Her shoes clip-clopped on the floor as she walked and she moved at quite a speed, as if she was late for a meeting. Billy followed, struggling to keep up.

The light was pouring through a doorway at the end of the corridor. As she approached the door she stopped. She knocked on the door four times, before entering and standing in front of it. Billy could see a large table shaped like an egg with some older looking people behind it. They were stern and angry looking.

He thought he could make out the back of a group of young people's heads, sat rather still on the other side of the table.

As he approached the door, his heart started beating out of his chest and he was struggling to breathe. He could feel himself sweating. He gulped, took a step inside and... woke up.

FOUR

The first thing Billy did, every morning, before he faced the world, was reach for his hearing aid. It was a small skin-coloured device and very effective. The device was commonplace now for those who were born with a condition called microtia. It was the cause of the Demon Dinner Lady and everybody else shouting at him all of the time, despite Mum and Dad reminding people that they only needed to speak at normal volumes.

Billy was used to it. He'd grown up with it. He'd had several operations and it was all like second nature now. A few people had asked questions at school, but there was only one occasion where he was picked on and he'd steered clear of Rihanna and her gaggle of annoying mates ever since.

As he was coming down the stairs, he could hear his Dad's voice. It sounded so bizarre, like he was briefing his Mum on his forthcoming day, running through everything that was going on.

'Then of course at two thirty, I'll be picking up my car from its service and then at four o'clock I have a meeting with Adrian.' Dad said in rather a boring voice.

Billy walked into the kitchen. His Dad was holding a

newspaper up in front of his face. His Mum had her back to Dad, buttering some toast and staring out at the garden through the window.

'If Adrian thinks I'm going to go back on my word he's got another thing coming. Where is Billy? Another "can't be bothered to go to school" day, no doubt.'

Billy stared in absolute amazement. 'I'm here,' he half shouted.

'Good morning Son, how did you sleep?' Dad was smiling now and had placed the paper on the table, folding it carefully.

'Pretty badly, actually. Kept waking up, strange dreams.'

'It'll have something to do with the EMC249, I'm speaking today to the police. I've HAD ENOUGH.'

Billy stopped. He had no idea what was happening. Dad was speaking, but his mouth wasn't moving at all.

'Here's your toast dear,' Mum said, placing a plate down on the table opposite Dad. After turning away, Billy heard her voice again, 'that boy looks as white as a ghost, he must be coming down with something. Should I take his temperature? He can't go to school looking like that.'

Billy thought he was losing his mind. His Mum turned around again whilst she was making sound, but her lips weren't moving either.

'I just need a minute!' Billy exclaimed and ran back down the hallway and up the stairs, hearing his Mum saying 'Are you alright...?' followed swiftly by, 'I knew it. High temperature. He's ill.'

He got to the top of the stairs at record pace and raced back to his room. He shut his door and breathlessly turned and slid down the door. He whispered out loud 'What's happening to me?' He put his head in his hands and then started pinching his face to check he wasn't asleep.

Seconds later, he heard somebody approaching the door. 'I'd better knock, in case he's naked,' he heard. There were three knocks on the door and Billy leapt over to his bed and threw the covers over himself. He heard the door open. 'Right. Let's work out how ill he actually is. I really could do without him taking the day off...Are you alright Billy?'

'No,' Billy said quickly. 'I'm really ill, I need to take the day off.'

'Oh darling,' Mum said in a sickly sweet voice. 'What's wrong?'

Billy searched in his mind for symptoms. Mum said he'd looked pale.

'I feel sick, Mum. And, headache. I've got a headache.'

The second bit was too hesitant, he knew that he'd blown it immediately.

'Too hesitant,' he heard Mum's voice say, 'he's lying.'

'I'm not lying' Billy spat the words out so quickly that his Mum was startled and stopped suddenly.

'I didn't say you were darling, but here's what I think you should do. I think you should go in to school and see how you get on.'

'Okay, okay,' Billy replied. 'I'll be...I'll be down in a minute.'

He stayed under the covers and heard Mum close the door. It was official. He couldn't believe how or why it was possible, but he could hear what was going on inside of their heads.

FIVE

In the car on the way to school, he continued to hear his Dad's thoughts. He had worked out something positive. He had to be focused on the person for it to happen. As they drove through the curvy narrow streets on the way to school, he had passed many people that he could see outside of the car window.

He couldn't hear anything at all. He tested this by fixating on a man at the bus stop. As he did so, he started to hear a song that the gentleman was humming in his head. 'Yesterday, all my troubles Dee Dee Dee.' As soon as he removed his focus from him, the sound faded away almost immediately. What a relief, he thought.

When walking towards the school gates, his Dad patted him on the head and then walked off in the other direction, away from his car and towards the front entrance of the school.

The pupils used a different entrance. A small, rickety old gate, with rusty hinges. Over the summer, the school caretakers, Mr and Mrs Scratchnsniff, had done their best to paint over the dank wooden patches – but it had made it look worse.

For the record, Scratchnsniff was not their real name. A few years ago, Chloe Buckles had felt sick during morning reading and had been sent up to the medical room by Mrs Clinch. She swore blindly that the caretakers were scratching their eyebrows so much that little tufts of dandruff and dust were flying out of the air. In turn they were sniffing it and then eating it in the corridor. From that day forth, they were known as Mr and Mrs Scratchnsniff.

There was a hubbub of noise ringing through his ears, all sorts of weird and wonderful conversations from his friends, people who thought they were his friends and people who would definitely not be his friends under any circumstances. Mr Scratchnsniff was pruning roses by the student entrance to the school.

'I don't care, I don't care, I'm wearing women's underwear' he heard loudly as he walked past.

Billy stopped. He shot his head around to see Mr Scratchnsniff, minding his own business and clipping dead bits of rose into his hand. He looked up at Billy, who stepped back startled.

'Morning Fella' said Mr Scratchnsniff.

'Good morning Mr Scratch- I mean…Good morning Mister…Sir…Good morning Sir.'

'What are you so nervous about? It's just a rose bush. If you want to be really afraid, you should go and see the grass snake I found in the meadow. I nearly wet my knick…pants.'

Billy produced the fakest of smiles, the sort you give the dentist when they ask how you're feeling before they prod around your back molars. He tightened his backpack and walked into the school.

I need to stop focusing on people, he thought to himself. That way, I can't hear their thoughts.

SIX

Over the next few days, Billy found the worst time was lunch time.

The noise is unbearable at the best of times. People talking with their mouths full. The Demon Dinner Lady and her persistent shouting. Constant bits of potato and rice pudding flying across the room while people discussed the brilliant film they watched the previous evening, or they told each other how much they hated their parents.

But for Billy, even trying not to hear made no difference. As soon as he focused on somebody, it was like he was holding up a doctor's stethoscope to their brain and hearing their thoughts amplified like a rock concert. Whatever they were thinking about that second, was alive ringing around his brain.

Nobody wants to hear that Rhys Smith needs the toilet when he's shovelling huge handfuls of lettuce into his mouth and munching on it like a rabbit.

Nobody wants to hear that Gloria Rangleford wet herself the previous evening whilst she was drinking, not from the little blue plastic cups like everybody else, but from the jug in the middle of the table.

Out of the corner of his eye, he noticed the Headmistress

appear in the hall doorway. Her lips were not moving, but he could distinctly hear his name being spoken in her voice, as her eyes darted around the room.

As they made eye contact, he heard a loud 'there he is' and she started moving towards him. She leant down at the table and her necklace dropped into his gravy. The table fell silent. As Billy looked around the table he heard several of his classmates' thoughts.

Thank goodness it isn't me, thought one. What has Billy done? thought another. I hope this is not about yesterday when I tried to flush that crisp packet down the bogs and blocked the entire thing, thought Danny, sat at the end of the table.

Billy could feel his face burning as he looked down to see the Headmistress's necklace dangling between his mashed potato and gravy.

'Billy, could you follow me please.' she said.

Billy's getting expelled, thought one friend at the table. We'll never see him again, thought another.

'As soon as you can, chop-chop.' The Headmistress did a little clap and then stood up and walked towards the door, with mashed potato smeared all over her blouse and gravy dripping down on the floor from the base of her silver necklace.

Rather than listening to the others at the table offering him words of comfort, he stood up immediately with his legs shaking slightly and moved towards the door.

The reception area was quiet, so his ears were not talking to him for a short time. No other voices. He stood still for a moment, basking in the silence in the same way that you do with the sunshine when you step off an aeroplane in a hot country.

He took a deep breath, knocked on the door and stepped into the office.

SEVEN

He stepped inside and saw the Headmistress sat behind her desk, peering at her computer screen. She looked up at him instantly.

'Sit down, please' she said to him. Her voice was stern but unusually kind.

He sat on the seat on the other side of her desk, which seemed far less comfortable than the chair she was sitting in. Lovely cream leather with a high back. It felt like the chair he was sat on was just stolen from a classroom. Maybe, he thought, it's so that parents don't stay very long in awkward meetings. It could also be because she didn't want people to feel comfortable when they were being told off.

At some point in the last few minutes, the Headmistress must have noticed the gravy and mashed potato on her top and had tried to scrub it off with a tissue because Billy noticed there were tiny flaky bits of tissue paper stuck to her like glue.

The Headmistress stared at him for what seemed like twenty minutes.

At home, Billy would have said something sarcastic like 'Are you feeling alright?' but he thought better of it. He might already be getting told off as it is, he did not want to add to her fury.

'How are you Billy?'

'I'm...fine thanks. How are you?'

Her lips did not move and he heard 'I hate my job!' as a loud shout, which made him wince and put his hand toward his ear, ready to shield.

'I'm very well indeed, thank you. Now, how was the test?'

Why were people so fascinated and intrigued by this test, he thought. More importantly, why had she chosen him to conduct her secret questionnaire?

'It was fine, thank you.' he said hesitantly.

'It seems you must have done very well.' she said, smiling a little, although Billy was sure the smile was sarcastic and not genuine.

'Seems? What do you mean? Why?' Billy asked.

The Headmistress leant to the left-hand side and wobbled like a jelly as she moved her arm to open her top desk drawer and pulled out a little brown box. His name was written on the top of the box.

'This came for you' she said.

She explained that a telephone call had come beforehand to tell her it was on its way. Owing to security, only the child named on the envelope was allowed to open it and to check it was not anything awful, a teacher was allowed to be present whilst the student read the enclosed letter to themselves. That said, they were not, under any circumstances, allowed to open the box until they were by themselves.

Billy shuddered. Why him, why now? He was so happy with his life and his parents and his small group of friends. He was so nervous by all of this and vowed to himself that he would never again moan about anything if only all of this would just disappear and he could go back to normal. The

way things were a week ago.

'I've only agreed to all of this, because the Prime Minister telephoned me personally this morning.' said the Headmistress.

'Agreed to what?' asked Billy.

'Agreed to allow you to open this and read the letter. I have to have evidence that I've not seen what's inside the box by asking you to sign this form.'

She pulled out another piece of paper from the top drawer and placed it onto the table.

'So go on,' she said. 'Open up the parcel, read the accompanying letter but do not open the box until you get home.'

Billy cautiously opened up the letter and began to read. It was so awkward, trying to concentrate when he knew the Headmistress was staring at him.

'Dear Billy,

Congratulations. You are one of the VERY elite few. If you do not know what that means, you soon will do.

Contained in this box is a device that will unlock the key to your glorious future. Keep it safe, do not show anybody, use the charger provided and keep it plugged in secretly at all times.

This is top secret, and this comes as an order from the British Government.

Yours sincerely,

The Prime Minister.'

He looked up at the Headmistress who was sitting there, with a face like she had sucked the biggest lemon in the world. He could see that she was desperately trying to decipher exactly what was in the contents of the letter. Billy gave a little nod as if he had understood what was written inside and looked back at her. All of a sudden, he felt quite sorry for her. Teachers had all the power, teachers had all the rights, teachers could tell you where to go and what to do...Teachers could even tell you which toilets you were allowed to use! But in this instance, Billy felt like the most powerful boy in the world. In his hand, was the biggest secret in the school, possibly even the biggest secret in the country. He had been chosen for something by the Prime Minister.

He made the most out of this moment, by folding the piece of paper very carefully into four. Then he folded it again. He placed it in the top pocket of his polo shirt and picked up the small brown parcel.

'You should probably hide that,' the Headmistress said, adding, 'I've got a bag you can put it in.'

She smiled at him all of a sudden and became like a warm, fuzzy grandmother. Billy could not believe his thinking, but he wanted to walk around to her and give her the biggest hug, before realising that this thought was absolutely vile and disgusting. The Headmistress removed a few items from a brown paper bag and handed it to him.

'Here you are.' she said.

'Thank you.' Billy replied, quickly placing the small parcel into the bag.

He stood up from his uncomfortable chair and straightened his back, turning to walk towards the door. All of a sudden, he froze and then turned back to his Headmistress.

'What do I do when everybody asks me why I was here?'

The Headmistress looked across at the wall, realising that persuading Billy to lie was a bad thing. She pondered and opened her mouth to speak several times and then stopped herself.

'Given the nature of this,' she exclaimed 'I think you should just tell everyone you forgot your PE kit for the cross country run this afternoon.'

The blood drained from Billy's face. He had planned to pretend he had forgotten his PE kit before the cross-country run anyway. Long gone were the days when teachers could make you do PE in your pants and vest if you had forgotten your kit, so it was a lie that never failed. Billy had realised that if you did it less than three times a term, it was not even mentioned at parents' evenings or on your end of year report. The huge cross-country run was going to be one of those occasions. Now he was going to have to run every step of it – to keep this huge lie a reality.

'Thank you Miss,' Billy said gulping and turning back towards the door.

'Whatever this is,' the Headmistress replied, 'do let me know how you get on.'

Billy opened the door and stepped back into the corridor. As he went to close the door behind him, the still mouth of the Headmistress seemed to speak in a sarcastic tone that he'd never heard before. 'Fancy not telling the head teacher of the school, stupid blinking government.'

She gave him a sickly smile and he tried not to reveal that he could hear what she was thinking as he closed the door behind him.

EIGHT

Billy did not come last in the cross-country race. The next few hours went as follows:

Brown bag in backpack
PE kit on
Outside, running like mad
Getting soaked
Dodging puddles
Out of breath
School uniform on
School bell
Picked up by Mum
Up the stairs and back in his bedroom.

He took the brown paper bag out of his rucksack and placed it on his bed. He walked back over to his bedroom door and opened it, checking there was nobody on the landing.

He laid down on his bed, with the bag in front of him. He studied it, like he was staring at an artefact in a museum. It wasn't a particularly special box, just the sort you get in the post if you order something online. It was a perfect cube and about the size of a slice of pizza.

It was stuck together perfectly with brown parcel tape. Billy got up and grabbed his pair of scissors from his top drawer and prized them open. They were a babyish plastic kind of scissors and he was worried they would not be strong enough. With the scissors open, he cut down one side and then underneath the side flaps. He opened the top flap and inside there was a piece of foam that covered the entire surface of the box. He pinched it in the middle and pulled it out and underneath was a small, black piece of plastic. It was shaped like a square wristwatch, without the band. He lifted it out and held it in his hand. It fitted perfectly in the middle of his palm. Looking back down into the box, he could see what looked like a charger and a plug on the other side of it.

There was a plug socket behind his bed. After a bit of jiggling around with the bed frame, he managed to plug in the charger and found the place on the device that the other end perfectly slotted into.

Instantly, the device lit up with one word in the centre. 'Online.' That was it. No buttons, no options. He tried swiping it, throwing it, pressing it... In fact, he tried everything in the world, except eating it, but nothing happened. It just continued to say 'online.'

He placed it secretly underneath his pillow and joined his family downstairs.

Over dinner, he found it bizarre that he wasn't sharing the most important event of his life with his Mum and Dad. It was his favourite dinner: chicken Kiev, chips, baked beans and salad. Mum had even grated cheese over the beans and chips. The food put him in such a good mood that several times throughout the meal, he had to stop himself from telling them absolutely everything.

He turned his attention to cross-country and described every part of the course in absolute detail, to the point where his Mum and Dad were so bored. How did he know? He could HEAR it.

Why's he so interested in describing the puddle next to the goal post? Dad had thought, about two minutes in. Focus, focus, don't switch off, your boy is telling you about his day. Stop thinking about the chocolate cake in the fridge, Mum was thinking.

'Well darling,' Mum spoke out loud, 'it's so nice that you've shared so much of that cross-country run with us.'

'It seems we have a runner in the family,' Dad said. 'I'll have a look online and see if there are any running clubs on Saturdays' he added, 'it sounds like you could be our next long-distance gold medallist.'

Billy's face started to turn pale again. Cheese on chips and beans was not that brilliant after all.

For the first time in his life, Billy was absolutely desperate to go to bed. He had a few more ideas about other ways to get the small device to say anything else but 'online' and had rushed upstairs to try them out throughout the course of the evening. Nothing whatsoever worked.

When it was eventually time for bed, he'd completely run out of options. He lay there, getting angrier and angrier. There was absolutely no way he was going to be able to fall asleep. There were not enough sheep or fences they could jump over to stop him from wondering what on earth this was all about. When he eventually did shut his eyes, finally thinking he might be able to drop off, his eyelids started shining in a bright colour. His eyes shot open and darted around the room looking for the light source. As his eyes wandered around, he noticed it was underneath his pillow. Blue, amber, red, blue, amber, red.

He grabbed the small black device and held it in his hand. The word 'online' had disappeared and had been replaced with 'tap once.' His fingers started to tremble as he moved his hand towards the device. He did as he was instructed and tapped the device gently in the centre.

Suddenly, the screen lit up brightly and he could see the face of a rather kind looking lady in the centre. She's the sort of person that is on the gate of a ride at a theme park. Full of smiles and an excited glint in her eye, like she knows that you're about to experience the best roller coaster in the world.

'Hello Billy' said the lady.

'Hello.'

'Nice pyjamas,' she said, smiling.

Billy looked down at the awful pyjamas he was wearing. Every year, without fail, his Grandmother would buy him the most hideous set of pyjamas that he would never choose to wear. He did everything in his power to hide them under every item of clothing in his drawers so that come Boxing Day, they would never be seen again. Every so often, when he had not done as his Mum had asked and put his dirty clothes in the wash bin, all that would be left was Grandma's Christmas pyjamas. Mum would make him wear them as punishment. This particular offering from Granny was bright purple with orange stripes down the arms.

'Sorry,' said Billy, his voice exploding at the device.

'Sssssh,' interrupted the lady, 'don't wake anybody else in the house. We need you to come to Downing Street, Billy.'

'Ok, tell me when and I'll get my Dad to drive me.' Billy replied.

'There's no time for that, Billy. We need you here at 2am.' she said quickly.

'What time is it now?' Billy asked.

'It's eleven thirty.'

'But...I...we live an hour away from London. I'll never make it on time.'

'Don't worry Billy, we're sending a car for you. It will be outside your house at 12:30.'

'But I've got school in the morning.'

'Don't worry about anything like that. We'll sort it out for you.'

'But, but-'

Billy was trying to think of something to say, find an excuse, or work out how on earth he was going to get out of the front door without waking Mum and Dad.

'Now, Billy' said the lady with rosy cheeks, 'is there a way you can leave your bedroom not via the door?'

Billy looked at her like she had lost her mind.

'The only way,' he said, 'would be out of the-'

'Is there a window, for example?' she said, cutting him off mid-sentence.

'Well – yes, but-'

'Perfect. And is it safe to get down? What I mean to say is...Is there a way you can climb down safely?'

Billy remembered that there was a small pitched roof above the front porch directly below his window. Dad had once had a fake fire drill, asking him to make his way out of the bedroom via the window. He said he had done it to make sure that Billy knew a way to get out of the house safely, if his doorway was blocked and there was an emergency. Why, Billy thought, would anybody start a fire directly outside of my bedroom door?

***

'I can climb down, yes,' Billy said nervously.

'Excellent, be careful, do it at 12:25 so that you don't keep the driver waiting. See you when you get here...oh and maybe change those pyjamas Billy, you don't want the orange stripes to scare the police officer at the front door.'

Billy went to ask her a million more questions, but the screen went blank. Only to be replaced by the word 'online' again.

Did he need to take the device with him? What was he supposed to wear? Did he need to bring a bag? Something to write with? Should he clean his teeth as if it was the morning?

He grabbed his hearing aid from the bedside table and put it on quickly. He downed the glass of water next to his bed like he had run another cross-country race and pulled open his wardrobe doors to select an outfit.

Should he go smart, or casual? This was Ten Downing Street. The Prime Minister's house, for goodness sake. Maybe they will want to take photos or make a video? A smart polo shirt and pair of jeans should do it.

He was dressed, ready and good to go about two minutes after he had finished the chat with Rosy Cheeks, which meant, it was no later than eleven thirty-five. He did not know the exact time, the clock on his wall had run out of battery months ago. He could not go out onto the landing to check either.

Whenever cars came around the corner and it was dark outside, Billy could see a large shadow form across the back of his curtains. He often saw this when he got into bed. That is what he had been waiting for. Several shadows formed and then disappeared again. He was waiting for the shadow that stayed where it was, because the car would stop moving outside his house.

He had managed to keep all of this a secret. But he was

about to risk it all. For his bladder. He knew he needed a wee whilst he was talking to Rosy Cheeks. He also knew he would not be able to ask the driver to stop on the way to Downing Street, so his only option was to tiptoe down towards the bathroom.

The whole process felt like it took about twenty minutes. Billy had never moved so slowly, which when you are desperate for the toilet, is quite difficult to do. It was like torture, seeing the toilet less than twenty steps away across the hallway but moving so slowly to avoid all of the creaks in the floorboards. He just could not risk waking up Mum and Dad.

Eventually, he arrived at 'destination lavatory' and switched on the light. Two minutes later, he was on his way out again feeling relieved.

He heard some muttering and then footsteps padding from Mum and Dad's bedroom.

Oh no, thought Billy. This is it. It's okay, I'll be fine, he thought to himself. Anyone can need a wee in the night. Then his brain shouted at him, don't be so ridiculous, Billy. Anyone can wake up for a wee in the night, but not everyone puts their smartest clothes on to walk to the bathroom.

In the bathroom, Billy saw the airing cupboard door was open. Without thinking, he darted in there, jumping up onto the middle shelf. He moved some towels out of the way and covered himself. He grabbed the door and pulled it towards him and it creaked sharply.

It was boiling hot in there, like being in the middle of the Sahara Desert. The boiler made a deafening whirring sound, so much so that he had to cup his hand over his left ear, in a desperate attempt to mute his hearing aid.

Without going into details, hearing your Dad on the toilet in the middle of the night after eating three chicken Kievs, chips, beans, cheese and tomato sauce is not the most pleasant experience in the world. But Billy reassured himself that it was his only option. After Dad had left the bathroom, switching the light out on his way, Billy was left in the pitch black. No morsel of light was left to try and find his way silently out of the bathroom and back to his own room.

NINE

Billy was way past watching shadows on the curtains. He had drawn them wide open and could see the road outside his house. Only the scattered street lamps provided light. It's a weird sensation, Billy thought, standing in a dark room looking at light outside. It is like being in a cinema when the lights dim, just before the film begins.

He had the most bizarre feeling in his stomach too. Instead of butterflies, it felt as if there were snakes wriggling around in there. He tried to work out whether that meant he was excited or terrified and settled on a combination of the two.

A few minutes passed and eventually, a light flickered across the pavement. A beautiful black car turned into the road and made its way up towards Billy's house. The car was so grand and graceful, it was like a celebrity gliding up a red carpet towards him.

Billy walked over to his bedside lamp and switched it off and then slowly unlocked his bedroom window. He moved the silver lever to the right. Remembering his window had the most awful squeak when it opened, he gave it one sharp push to reduce the chances of waking Mum and Dad. It sounded like the sort of shriek you hear when you accidentally or on

purpose step on the tail of a cat, but it only lasted for a split second.

He pushed his body weight onto the windowsill and kicked his feet up, falling straight back down again, narrowly dodging his piggy bank and his 'Star of the Week' award from School a few years back. Mum had been so proud of him she had put the certificate in a frame. Billy remembered thinking that if she was that proud, she would have framed it and put it in the dining room cabinet with all of her best china.

He kicked up his feet again and made it this time, finding his balance when he reached the top. The distance from his window to the roof was about six feet, which meant he could not just step down. He would have to lower himself slowly, taking the weight on his arms until his feet touched the top of the roof.

Once he had done that, he realised that he needed to shut his bedroom window. That meant pulling himself back up, not fun at midnight in the outside air when nobody is supposed to know you are escaping from your own house.

He caught a glimpse of his neighbours, Fred and Frieda, across the street. They were in very old school nightgowns watching television. If I get spotted now, he thought, it's game over.

He shut the window quickly and lowered himself back down until he could feel the apex of the roof beneath his trainers. Still eight feet from the floor, he had three options.

Option 1: Jump.

Positives: it's over quickly, won't keep the driver waiting, least chance of making noise by landing on grass.

Negatives: Potential of breaking most bones in body, potential of screaming, potential of landing on head, potential of certain death.

Option 2: Use one of the four pillars as a firefighter pole.

Positives: Could be fun, never done it before, pole goes almost fully down to the ground.

Negatives: Billy is not a firefighter, he's had no pole dancing lessons, the pillar is square rather than round which could be painful, potential of certain death.

Option 3: Remove polo shirt, tie it to the top of the pillar and lower down as if abseiling.

Positives: It would feel the most like he was in a Hollywood film, he'd be able to control the speed and it would be relatively fast.

Negatives: Polo shirt could get stuck on the pillar (meaning he would meet the Prime Minister half naked), polo shirt could tear meaning that falling to the ground would be certain, potential of certain death.

So far, all three of the options could result in death. Before he even gave himself time to think, he jumped down from the top. Instead of landing and stumbling forwards, he found himself bunny hopping around the garden trying to get his balance back. Apart from pain up his shins when he first landed, he was pleased he managed to get down fully clothed and by avoiding death.

He gave a small wave to the driver and walked up towards the driver's window.

The window lowered very slowly and a man who looked like he had not shaved for three or four days turned his head towards him. He smiled at Billy and when he did so, a gold front tooth sparkled in the moonlight.

'Now tell me,' said the gentleman with the black tie 'what is a young lad doing out here at half past midnight?'

'Erm…I think you're giving me a lift to 10 Downing Street?' Billy looked up at him and smiled, he could have winked at him as if to say 'We both know why we're here' but he decided against it.

'Nope, not me young man. I'm here to pick up a lady at number 42.'

Billy's heart practically leapt out of his chest. He thought his hearing aid was playing tricks on him. His eyes went misty with panic and he grabbed hold of his head, worrying about what to do next.

'Oh…Oh my goodness, okay well…' Billy's voice trembled out of his mouth like a complete and utter mess.

'Only joking son,' smiled the smart gentleman, 'hop in.'

Billy's panic turned into a sense of relief and he rushed around to the other side of the car, opening the passenger door.

'No, no,' said the gentleman, 'you're being driven, you must sit in the back.'

Billy closed the door gently and then got into the back of the car.

'Where to then?' smiled the unshaven driver.

'Ten Downing Street please' Billy said back.

'Right you are, lad.'

The inside of the car was like a spaceship, there was even a little fridge in the middle. Billy could see cans of coke and sweets in there. There were dials and screens all over the place.

'Help yourself to whatever you like, courtesy of the Prime Minister,' said Mr Smart-Unshaven.

'Thank you very much,' said Billy, thinking about whether or not they'd have his favourite films to watch on one of the two screens.

With that, the celebrity-looking car roared away into the midnight air, leaving only a small puff of smoke rising up in front of his empty bedroom.

TEN

Billy could tell when they had reached central London. Everything seemed so much busier. The lights seemed to be a wash of blue. Blue fairy lights, blue lights around trees, big buildings lit up...in blue. He could not believe that a city could be so alive at half past one in the morning. There were people walking around, people in bars and restaurants. A newly married couple danced down the road holding hands. There was even one lady walking her dog. Billy wondered if the dog and owner spent their whole day asleep, only venturing out at night. Or maybe she was a vampire and she only came when it was dark? Even though it was busy, there was a stillness in the air. Not quite silence, but similar to it. Just a gentle breeze and the sound of cars and friendly chatter.

The car turned through an archway and then through some big black gates. Billy had seen this street several times on the news. Downing Street. He'd made it, to the Prime Minister's house. All of a sudden, those snakes returned, swirling around through all of the sweets and diet coke he had consumed over the last hour or so.

'Well, here we are Sonny' said Mr Nevershave.

'Thank you so much,' Billy replied.

Billy worried that he was supposed to give the man a tip. Dad always gave a tip to a taxi driver if they had been pleasant and kind throughout a journey. Not only had Mr Bitsofstubble been incredibly kind, he'd also provided Billy with snacks and drinks – something that he had never experienced before.

He searched around in his pockets, frantically looking for some coins or bits of shrapnel to offer to him. There was nothing there except a few paperclips and a marble. He felt embarrassed.

'Don't be nervous,' said Mr Needarazor, 'they'll look after you.'

And with that, the driver stepped out of the car and walked around it, opening the door for Billy.

'Very best of luck to you, lad.' he said, patting Billy on the shoulder. And with that, he got back into the car and drove off, leaving Billy stood outside 10 Downing Street.

He looked around for a knocker and a doorbell and could not see one. Given the time of night, Billy did not want to knock on the door, but it looked like that was the only option.

As he approached the doorway, the door gently opened. No squeaks here unlike his bedroom window, just a silent swing revealing a very long corridor. A lady popped into his sight and all of a sudden, he had a flashback to the dream he had a few nights before.

She was dressed like a head teacher, with jet black hair scraped back.

'You must be Billy,' she said.

'Yes, that's right,' Billy replied.

'You're looking a bit nervous, there's no need to be. Follow me please.'

And with that, she turned on her heels and started walking at quite a pace, just like in his dream. She was a lot kinder than she had been in his dream, less mysterious. Billy walked quickly to try and keep up.

The building was like a Tardis, it looked quite small from the outside. As Billy walked around the maze of corridors with huge pictures on the wall, he wondered how anybody who worked here did not spend their whole life getting lost?

The lady began to slow down in the murkiest of all of the corridors. In a small panel on the wall, she entered a code. Rather than the door opening, a small piece of metal lifted on the door revealing a hand shaped print.

Without hesitation, the lady placed her palm on the door and the doors separated in the centre. There was a large oval table in the centre of the room and Billy could see the backs of four other heads, sat in grand swivel chairs.

As he entered the room, all four of the heads turned towards him. They all seemed to be roughly the same age as him and they all had the same look of wonderment in their eyes, mixed with the same look of having snakes writhing around in their bellies.

'Take a seat,' said the kind, head teacher-looking lady.

'Alright then,' Billy replied nervously.

There was only one seat on this side of the table, and it was right in the centre. Billy looked around at the other four faces, pulled the chair out and sat down. It was warm, comfortable and all of a sudden, he felt a little calmer.

Almost immediately after he had sat down, he looked across at the other faces in the room and as he did so, heard them…but not out loud.

Well, it's not just about the face then, thought the girl on the end.

Damn it. I've forgotten my glasses, that's embarrassing, thought the second along.

Can I do my usual joke? thought the boy directly next to him.

And on the far-left hand side, the really shy looking boy thought, how am I going to prove it, if they ask me?

Before he had had a chance to even say hello or introduce himself out loud to the others, another door opened. In walked the Prime Minister. He was holding a red briefcase, which he placed down on the table and then he sat down. Two other ladies were with him and sat on either side.

He leant forward a little and spoke softly.

'Good morning everybody. It's so nice to meet you all. Normally, in these situations, I might be visiting you at school and you'd be telling me what you'd been up to. The school would've gone to a huge effort, spent lots of money because the Prime Minister was coming. Instead, I've asked you to come to my house.'

He let out a beaming smile. Billy thought he looked different from how he did on the TV. He looked less grand and less important. Just like a normal man, really.

'I know you're all probably feeling a mixture of excitement and terror.'

Without thinking, Billy nodded. As he looked around, the other four children were smiling and nodding too.

'Well, let me reassure you, there's nothing to be terrified of. You're in the safest hands here. You're here because each and every one of you are absolutely fantastic. More fantastic, in fact, than anybody else who's your age in the entire country.

Almost a week ago now, everybody in Year 6 across the country was given a test. With that test, came a bottle of water. Every single person who took the test across the country drank that water whilst they were doing the test.'

The Prime Minister lowered his gaze and looked around at

the five children, sitting there silently. Billy thought to himself, well, that's awkward, because I didn't drink the water during the test at all.

'All,' the Prime Minister continued 'except five people. Those five people are sitting in front of me now. Something stopped you, something deterred you from having one sip during the test although every single one of you has drunk the water since.'

Billy suddenly felt like he was part of a special team. The snakes in his stomach had disappeared now and had been replaced by a warm, bubbly feeling.

'As well as being the finest mineral water we could source from the beautiful highlands of Scotland, we got permission from the World Health Organisation to add a special substance to it. Parents and teachers across the land have been disgusted by this, because we kept it a secret. People have protested and called it an outrage.'

Billy remembered how cross his Dad was the morning after the test, at breakfast. He had heard him thinking...

'The substance, is called EMC249, which was developed by some absolutely brilliant minds at the University of Cambridge.'

Again, Billy thought of his Dad. He always said to Billy that he dreamt that one day, Billy would go to university at Oxford or Cambridge and do something a lot cleverer than he did.

The Prime Minister continued, slowing down for dramatic effect:

'EMC249 unlocks superhuman abilities. We took the data that everybody wrote down and studied how their answers were affected by drinking the water. Only five sets of answers across the entire country contained what we were looking for and most bizarrely, none of you needed to drink it. As you now all have, if you wouldn't mind, I'd like you to introduce yourselves one by one and describe what you've been feeling since.'

ELEVEN

A girl leant forward at the end of the table. It was natural for her to go first because she was at the end where the Prime Minister was looking.

'My name's Poppy.' she said. Billy noticed that she had a very slight lisp. You could only just make it out.

'Since drinking the water on the night of the test,' she added, 'I've been able to speak different languages. I don't know how many exactly, I've counted fourteen so far. It's the most bizarre thing, if I'm on a bus or a tube, as I am every morning on my way to school...I can understand everything people are saying. It really freaked me out at first, but now I'm used to it, I kind of like it.'

'Well,' said the Prime Minister, 'It's lovely to meet you Poppy.' His eyes moved along to a blond-haired girl to the right of Billy. She seemed a little more nervous than everybody else and her eyes squinted a little, every time the Prime Minister moved.

'I'm Gracie, I'm eleven. Since drinking the EMD4 thing, I can see through walls. It's been really odd, I was born colour blind so I've always struggled with seeing stuff.'

Poppy turned around to her and smiled. Gracie nervously

looked at her, as if to question her smile.

'I forgot to say' Poppy added, 'I was born with half a lip and so couldn't really speak until I was four even though I had a load of operations, my Mum says I just refused to speak. So being able to talk in different languages is super weird.'

Gracie smiled back at her and then looked forward at the Prime Minister.

'It's a pleasure to have you with us Gracie,' he said with a smile and then turned his gaze towards Billy.

'I'm er – I'm…I'm Billy. I'm nearly eleven. I was born with this rare condition…Microtia. It means my ear is a different shape and I struggle to hear. I've got my hearing aid. Since drinking the stuff, I've been able to hear people's thoughts…'

I bet he couldn't hear that I'd rather be in bed, I'm the most tired I've ever been, thought the woman to the left of the Prime Minister. Billy looked across at her, with a rising sense of confidence. More confident than he had been up until this point.

'I'm sorry you're the most tired you've ever been.' Billy said to her.

The woman's face dropped. Her mouth opened wide and she blinked three times incredibly fast.

'Good Lord,' the woman said, out loud, 'that's extraordinary.'

'Thanks for being here with us Billy,' said the Prime Minister and then turning to his colleague he smiled and added, 'sorry for keeping you up Marjorie.'

'I'm sorry Sir,' she replied. 'I meant to think that…I mean I did think tha…Never mind.'

To Billy's immediate left was a boy called Max.

'I'm Max, I was eleven on September 6th. I was born with a thing that means I don't have a right arm, but don't worry…

I'm 'armless.'

All three of the Government people laughed out loud hysterically. Billy looked around and all of the kids were laughing too, including Max, so he let out a giggle.

'Since I drank it,' Max continued, 'I've been able to lift things with my left arm...'

'Couldn't you before?' the Prime Minister asked.

'Yes, of course I could lift the things that you could lift. But I mean, bigger things.'

'How big?' said the Prime Minister.

'Last night, I went out to get some stuff I'd left in my Mum's car. I leant on the handbrake. When I got out, the car started rolling backwards on the driveway. So I panicked (seriously, I nearly wet myself), I grabbed the door frame, stopped the car and pushed it back into place.'

'Extraordinary,' the Prime Minister replied, 'well, it's a real pleasure to have you here Max.'

The final young man at the end was smiling away at everybody's stories. Billy thought he had the sort of face that makes you want to be friends with him. A face filled with kindness and goodness, that is so rare for someone of his age.

'I feel a bit weird,' Freddie said. 'I wasn't born with anything like that. I just drank that stuff and all of a sudden, I can just disappear. I know it sounds weird, well, it is weird. If I feel like I need to, I can literally disappear.'

'Invisibility?' the Prime Minister asked.

'Yes, I think so. But it's been a weird one to test, because I can't do it when anybody is looking at me, or even in the same room. I have to be by myself and it has to be dark.'

Billy felt the weirdest he had ever felt in his life. There he was, with all of these voices blaring around his head for the last few days and all of a sudden, he realised that there were other people his age who had experienced exactly the same thing. It made him feel really secure, like he could finally express himself in a way he never had before.

'Thank you so very much for taking the time to introduce yourselves.' the Prime Minister said. 'Now, I won't leave the suspense of why you're all here building any longer. Although these extraordinary abilities are amazing and wonderful, the point is not to put you through a series of weird and bizarre experiments. In fact, we want to use these superb features you've all realised you have, to help us here as part of the government.'

Billy felt a sense of relief and as he looked around the room, he saw everybody else's shoulders lower and relax too. Whilst he had no idea what this little group was doing here, as everybody was introducing their superpowers, he suddenly panicked that women and men in white coats would be asking endless questions and he saw himself being hooked up to monitors and computers of every description.

'I'm sure you've all heard of MI5. They do extraordinary work to protect our country and keep us safe. What I have in front of me here,' the Prime Minister smiled, 'is the MI9.'

Nobody knew what this meant, but the general feeling was that it was something special.

'There are some things that adults just cannot do as well as children can,' the Prime Minister added. 'Things have come up recently, shall we say, that have made it difficult for the MI5 to carry out their duties effectively.'

Billy honestly had no idea what this meant and as he looked around, his newfound young colleagues looked equally baffled.

'I can't say too much more at the moment, as we're waiting for some more information. All I would say is, I'm very glad you're here. Those little devices you were given are essential for us being able to get in touch with you, so keep them with you at all times.'

All of the young people around the table started nodding in agreement.

'You're going to be working together quite closely, so in my opinion, you should spend the next few hours getting to know each other before heading home and getting some well-earned sleep. Now, no doubt we will meet again soon. I have a day full of meetings tomorrow, so alas, I must go to bed. Thank you all so much for being here and for your time.'

And with that, the Prime Minister got up from the table, beamed at the newly founded MI9, turned around and walked out of the room.

'Right, who's hungry?' said the lady who had not previously spoken, then she pressed an intercom button on the table and added, 'Jeremy, we're ready for the food now.'

Over the course of the next ten minutes, every takeaway food you could possibly imagine was brought into the room - burgers, chips, fizzy drink, pizza, Chinese, curry and chocolate.

'Now, tuck in!' the previously silent lady said. 'The cars will be back to pick you up at 3:30am and take you home. Take some time to get to know one another and enjoy the food.'

The two ladies smiled at each other and stood up in perfect unison, straightening their skirts and walking out of the room.

The five superheroes sat, eyes wide, completely silent, staring at one another.

TWELVE

Time seems like the weirdest thing sometimes. In a maths class at school, time seems to drag on like a tortoise trying to walk up Mount Everest. But when you are having a brilliant time, although it does not actually move any faster, time flies like a supersonic jet going from your house to the next door neighbours.

Billy thought that meeting these four new friends was more supersonic jet than Mount-Everest-tortoise.

Although it was gone three o'clock in the morning and the world outside was completely asleep, none of the five wanted to go home.

Whilst eating the biggest slice of pizza, Poppy made everybody laugh by telling a story of her experience the day before on the tube. Two school lads on a French exchange were talking about how much they fancied another girl opposite them. They spoke about her beautiful hair, gorgeous smile and how they just wanted to walk over and kiss her, right that second.

After that, speaking in their native tongue, the two of them said 'Dieu merci, personne ne nous comprend.' ('Thank goodness nobody understands us.')

The pretty girl looked up from her book and said, 'En fait, je suis française. J'ai entendu tout ce que tu as dit.' ('Actually, I'm French. I heard everything you said.')

The old lady with the bike next to the boys said 'Je parle aussi Francais' ('I speak French too.') And the two gentleman sat opposite them and Poppy all turned around and said 'Oui, nous vous avons entendu aussi' ('Yes, we heard you too.')

Poppy described the French boys' faces as turning a deep shade of red and purple and one of them was so embarrassed, he covered his eyes with his hands. They both rushed off the train at the next stop, like a reception student running for the toilet after assembly.

Billy was listening to them all in a way he hadn't before. The noises in his ears, hearing other people's thoughts out loud, was completely controllable. If he wanted to focus on somebody to discover what they were thinking, he could do so by focusing on them and tuning in to their brain. If he had no desire to hear it, he wouldn't have to.

'What did you write for the last question on the test at school?' Max said, eating a huge mouthful of pepperoni pizza.

'Eat that mouthful of food first.' replied Gracie, disgusted.

Silence fell over the group for the first time and all of them felt too embarrassed to say. Billy had forgotten the last question.

'What was it?' Billy asked.

'If you had one superpower what would it be?' Holly replied.

Billy knew instantly what his answer was, and he was too embarrassed to share the five words he'd written down.

'Mine was only five words.' Poppy said.

'Yeah, mine too,' added Freddie. 'Other people in my class wrote four paragraphs.'

Billy took a breath, plucked up the courage and started talking. All the others joined in, like a cheesy American game show:

'I'm happy how I am.'

Mrs NotTalkMuch came back and told everybody that their cars had arrived and it was time to leave.

Billy's ex-driver, Mr Whiskers, had been replaced by an older and much grumpier man, with no cans of coke in his car and no chewy sweets. Having said goodbye to all of his new friends, he shut one eye and then the other and before he knew it, he was waving goodbye to Mr GrumpyNightShift, climbing the pillar underneath his window, crawling into bed and laying still.

It was gone 4:30am and in just three hours, Billy would be putting on his school uniform like any other Year 6 school goer across the country.

The clever people at the University of Cambridge had come up with a pure solution of EMC249 which had been given to each of the five children in a small plastic bottle. Apparently, one sip would replenish any tiredness from the late-night meeting and allow each of the five to function normally for the remainder of the day.

When he lay there, taking off his hearing aid and staring at the ceiling, he played back through the most incredible night of his life. When he retold himself what had happened and allowed himself to think how his life had changed, he felt like he had something in his eye. His eyes clouded and as he gave them a quick rub, several tears smeared onto his cheek.

So that's what Mum meant when she said she was crying happy tears, he thought.

Turning over to one side, he eventually fell back to sleep again.

THIRTEEN

The radio came on at 7am sharp in Mum and Dad's room. Dad always had the radio on in the morning when he was getting ready.

In Billy's head, radio stations went as follows:

If you're young, it's radio 1

If you're old, it's radio 2

If you play a classical instrument, it's radio 3

If you're ancient, it's radio 4

But Dad listened to a local station because his friend Dave from school presented the breakfast show.

Billy remembered going over for a barbecue at their house earlier in the year and said to his Dad quietly, 'Why does he always talk like he's presenting a radio programme?'

'Ssssh, be quiet Billy. That's just the way he is,' Dad replied.

'And coming up at 3:30pm, we've got the burger buns arriving, hot from the supermarket shelves. Before that, it's cold drinks and chat, with me, David Simpson.'

When he was asking Billy about school (that is all that boring, non-interested grown ups can do) he felt like he was being interviewed on his radio programme:

'So tell me Billy, do you prefer Maths, English or Science? What's your favourite subject?'

'Erm... none of them really...'

'What's your teacher's name?'

'Errrr - Mrs Clinch.'

'And have you got a message for Mrs Clinch? Something you want to say to her?'

'Erm - no not really' Billy said, 'I see her most days.'

'Ah, that's a pity. Well, big shout out to Mrs Clinch anyway. Hope she's having a great day wherever she is.'

It made Billy's toes curl inside his shoes. Mum was polite and kind at the barbecue but when Billy asked what she thought about Dave the following morning she said:

'Your Dad had some weird friends at school, Billy.'

This particular morning, Billy didn't find Dave Simpson annoying at all. He was still so engrossed by the most important night of his life. He leapt out of bed and started dancing to one of Dave's morning choices.

'When you've been fighting for it all your life

You've been struggling to make things right

That's how a superhero learns to fly

Every day, every hour, turn the pain into power'

Billy had never danced before in his life, but there he was, standing in front of his bedroom mirror wearing Grandma's Christmas pyjamas, the ones she bought him, not hers, that would be creepy.

He started popping his knees forward and throwing his arms in the air and then without warning, he started twerking by squatting and sticking his bum out, shaking it around. With his newfound confidence he shut his eyes and danced away for the next few minutes.

He knew his next job was cleaning teeth, so with one final

twerking jump he leapt towards his bedroom door, throwing his arms in the air and opening his eyes like he'd scored the winning goal at Wembley.

Mum stood in the doorway and Billy instantly let out a yawn to try and cover up his dance moves.

'How long have you been stood there?' he asked her.

'Ages,' she replied smiling. 'I'll have to tell Dad to forget the running club, it seems we have a dancer in the family.'

'Shut up Mum.'

She smiled and turned away, before adding, 'Don't be rude, Billy.'

Although Billy was incredibly excited, the thought of an entire day's schooling made him feel absolutely exhausted, so he grabbed a quick swig of EMC249 from the little bottle he had been given and within a few minutes, he felt as good as new.

FOURTEEN

Life at school was just the same. The bullies still tried to steal lunch money, people got frustrated with the teachers and Billy could still hear other people's thoughts if he focused on them.

This was particularly useful if he wanted to know what people were thinking and came in especially useful with the answers for tests. It's amazing, thought Billy, how many teachers think of the answer to a question when they're reading the test out loud.

He'd grabbed his rucksack as usual and remembered he had to walk the mile home today, as Mum and Dad both had boring work stuff happening.

When he turned around the corner from the school gate, he noticed Mr Scratchnsniff mowing the school lawn and walking around the corner again, he noticed Chuck and Harry, the school bullies.

They had Danny from his class held up by his ankles, shaking him in the air. The entire contents of Danny's pockets were scattering all over the floor. There were a few fruit pastels, some coins, a bus pass and a few football cards.

Without thinking Billy bellowed 'Put him down!' as he ran as fast as he could over to where the bullies were.

The bullies dropped Danny immediately and turned around startled. Billy stared at them, deep into their eyes and tuned into their brains.

How ridiculous, thought Chuck, this measly, squirt, this stupid worm, this absolutely vile year six is sticking up for his pathetic friend. I'm going to turn him upside down, I'm going to punch his lights out, the first thing that I'm going to do is walk over to where he is and grab him by his collar.

As Chuck took the first step forward, Billy put his hand out in front of him and screamed 'STOP!' Chuck and Harry were so startled that they did stop.

'I know what you're thinking,' said Billy.

'Oh yeah?' barked Harry.

'What's that then you little worm?' added Chuck.

'You thought to yourself, he's sticking up for his pathetic friend. You were going to walk over and grab me by the collar. Then you were going to punch my lights out. Then, you thought you'd turn me upside down. So, now I've told you what you're going to do, you're going to have to rethink.'

There was a silence. Chuck and Harry did not move.

Chuck whispered to Harry, 'There's something creepy about that. What he just said, is exactly what I was just thinking, like, almost word for word.'

'That's what we always do,' Harry replied.

'I know, I know, but – that was pretty perfect, his guessing I mean.'

'What, you think he can hear inside your head?' said Harry, breaking out into a smile, 'Alright, pea-brain, I'm thinking of a number between one and a thousand, what number is it?'

Billy looked at him. He focused, there were a few things going on around Harry's brain but a number between one and a thousand certainly was not one of them.

'You're not thinking of one, probably so that, with the very small possibility that I would guess your number between one and a thousand, you could still say I was wrong. You were thinking about what you were having for tea and that the reason you can't control your temper is because your Mum and Dad are breaking up and it's made you so cross.'

Harry stared at him, his jaw fell open a bit and a little bit of dribble fell out of the corner of his mouth and down onto his chin. His eyes filled with tears.

'Get out of here. Now!' Harry screamed at him.

Billy stood still and folded his arms.

'I will,' he said 'but if I go, I want you to stop picking on people because you can't handle your own problems. It's pathetic and even though most people at school are scared of you, they're also bored of you.'

And with that, he helped Danny up from the floor. Danny had been silent the whole time and was gathering up the bits and pieces from his pockets. He was just pleased he'd managed to keep his pocket money and had escaped a beating.

Billy and Danny walked off and Billy tapped him on the shoulder, in a half reassuring and half comforting way.

'How did you do that?' asked Danny.

'Most of it was a lucky guess,' smiled Billy. 'His Mum cuts my Mum's hair and I heard her telling my Dad at the dinner table that she broke down in tears about breaking up with his Dad.'

'You're a genius.' Danny said.

'No, not a genius. Definitely not that.'

'Thank you anyway,' Danny replied, 'I owe you one.'

'Have a good evening' said Billy.

With that, he walked the mile or so home and could barely change the smile beaming from his face.

FIFTEEN

It was just before bedtime. If Dad fell asleep in front of the TV, Billy could sometimes get away with an extra few minutes sat watching one of the later night programmes that technically, he was not allowed to watch.

Tonight, Dad was asleep and Billy was channel hopping between programmes. In-between swapping from one channel to the next, there was a millisecond silence. In that brief pause, Billy could hear a weird scratching and buzzing noise.

He pressed pause on the TV and the noise did not go away. It was not getting any louder or quieter, it stayed exactly the same.

A thought came into his mind and he dashed upstairs. Sure enough, the black tiny thing buzzed away with the same 'tap anywhere' in the centre of the screen.

He stuck his head outside into the hallway and could hear the distant tones of Dad's snores coming from the living room. He shut his door quietly and tapped in the centre of the screen.

He smiled at the rosy-cheeked woman in the picture.

'Hi Billy, sorry it's late again. Glad you're still up.' she said.

'I was just off to bed soon.' smiled Billy.

'Not tonight I'm afraid Billy, the Prime Minister needs you here. All five of you. It's urgent.'

'Is this our first mission?'

'I'm afraid I can't say anymore Billy. The car will pick you up at midnight. Will the coast be clear then?'

'Should be fine' Billy whispered.

With that Rosy Cheeks put her thumb up on the screen before turning simply into the word 'online' once again.

Billy lay back onto the bed, completely relaxed and smiled away to himself.

The next few hours went as follows:

Wait for Dad to go to bed
Wait for Dad to fall asleep again in bed
Go to the toilet before getting changed
Put on smart chinos and polo shirt
Climb down from window
Drive to Downing Street
Walk through maze of corridors
Say 'Hi' to the four others
Eat some pizza
Wait for the Prime Minister to arrive

SIXTEEN

'Thanks for getting here so quickly,' said the Prime Minister smiling at them all. 'Would any of you happen to know what I meant when I said the word biofuel?'

The five of them shook their heads, completely clueless.

The Prime Minister sucked his teeth a little and his smile turned into a frown.

'In a nutshell,' he said quietly for more dramatic effect, 'biofuel is what every country in the world wants to be producing lots of but is unable to yet for various reasons.'

'Is it a type of petrol?' Freddie asked.

'Very much so,' answered the Prime Minister immediately, 'it comes from a thing called biomass – which is plant based, algae type material or animal waste.'

'Cow poo basically?' asked Poppy.

'Exactly,' the PM replied. 'The main reason why we want to use it to power all the cars on the road is that it is a source of renewable energy. Much kinder to the environment and can be mass produced much cheaper than the price of oil, coal and gas.'

There was an uncomfortable silence, that nobody seemed to want to break, although all five of them were sat there wondering the same thing. Billy, who hadn't said anything at all yet, eventually broke the silence.

'So how does this involve us?'

'Good question Bill,' replied the Prime Minister. 'Like I said to you all the other night, there are things the MI5 just cannot do because it's not practical. We've been gathering the intelligence on this for a while now and it seems we have to move quickly.'

Holly was getting impatient now. 'Just tell us,' she said 'we can handle it.'

'Perfect attitude Holly,' the PM said proudly. 'That's exactly why it was important we got the very best band of young people together. There is a school in West Sussex.'

Billy thought to himself, there are many schools in West Sussex, he would know – he lived there.

'It's an independent school, meaning that parents pay fees for their kids to go there. This particular school, Finian's Fields Manor, is run by a rather odd and sketchy gentleman called Phillip Crankbottom.'

Freddie and Poppy burst out laughing.

'I know, I know' said the PM. 'A rather unfortunate name for a headmaster.' He continued 'Intelligence has reached us, that they have come up with the formula for the mass production of this particular kind of biofuel and are about to roll it out across the country. We asked to work with them and share their ideas, but they wouldn't listen. There are two issues with this. If they go to the newspapers and TV stations with this and do it behind the country's back, they will make money that won't include the government which is highly illegal. We put taxes on fuel you see and if they do not do this, then they will make billions of pounds incredibly quickly and may sell it to one or more big corporations that sell petrol and diesel.'

Gracie had not opened her mouth yet but had been listening intently. 'Can't you just make a law to make it illegal?'

The Prime Minister looked at her. 'An excellent point,' he said adding, 'it's not quite that simple, because technically, we need to prove that they're doing something wrong first. And we can't because we have no evidence that they're doing anything at all.'

'What do you expect us to do to help?' Billy asked.

He thought to himself, it's bizarre how confident five young people were asking all these questions of the Prime Minister. A week ago, he was just a figure on TV and now they were interrupting him, asking lots of questions... Imagine if everybody did this at school all the time? Teachers would never be able to get through a single sentence, without being asked fifty-five million questions.

'An excellent question, Billy. But wait – there's more. In addition to all of this fuel stuff they're doing, they've come up with a formula – a recipe if you like, where food packaging, the sort you can buy in shops, can then be fed to animals.'

'Urgh,' Holly said, with a gasp, 'they're making them eat plastic?'

'No Holly, this is exactly my point. This is not plastic we're talking about here, it's animal feed made into packaging, the sort of stuff you'd feed a horse or a cow.'

'What, so, the packaging that you buy meals in at the shops,' Billy said, 'they've made one that can be fed to animals?'

'That,' the Prime Minister replied, 'is what our intelligence is suggesting, so, here's where you five come in to all this.'

Five young superhero heads leant forwards to hear the next instruction. Billy's heart started beating so loudly that he thought it was going to jump out onto the table and wave hello to everybody.

'I would like you to go undercover.'

The five heads suddenly all smiled at once. This was it. The call they had been waiting for, less than a week from taking a stupid test at school, here they were about to go undercover on behalf of the Prime Minister.

'You will all become students at Finian's Field Manor School, as soon as we can get you in there. My excellent team have been working flat out to enquire about places for you all, posing as your parents. We've created a means for you to arrive one by one at the school and have a short interview with the Headmaster.'

'Mr Crankbottom?' asked Freddie.

'Exactly. My team and I have come up with believable stories for why each of you would be joining midterm and so that's what I'd like you to do.'

'Do the kids who go there know what's going on?' asked Gracie.

'Almost certainly' the Prime Minister said, almost in a whisper. 'Our intelligence tells us that their press conference is next Thursday, so we have to find out the secret formula to the biofuel and the edible packaging before then and get you all out of there safely, in one piece. We have to go to the newspapers and TV stations before they do and expose them for who they really are.'

'Won't Mr CrankyBottomy – or whatever his name is – get suspicious that we're all arriving at once, a week before they go to do their press thingy?' Billy asked.

'Unfortunately,' the Prime Minister replied, 'this is a risk we will have to take if we're to stand any chance of getting this information.'

SEVENTEEN

Several hours of instructions and advice came after that. What each superhero's story was and how they would avoid being discovered and found out, during their short stay at Finian's Field Manor School.

Everybody's main concern is what their families would be told about where they were.

Billy was afraid that Mum and Dad would think he had just disappeared off the face of the earth and would not be lying peacefully in his bed as normal, when Dave Simpson came on the radio in the morning.

'Don't worry about anything like that,' said the Prime Minister. 'A government representative will be at your parents' front doors first thing in the morning, explaining everything to them. We will have to ask them to sign a disclaimer form to prevent them from telling anybody else, but they will be made aware that you're all safe and well and they will be told they can call anytime for an update on your health and wellbeing.'

Billy felt relieved by this, but he knew it would not stop his Mum from worrying about him.

'Will we be able to call home?' Billy asked.

'I'm afraid not Bill,' said the PM, 'it's essential that this is kept strictly as private government business.'

One by one, the young heroes were taken into a large meeting room, that had been filled top to bottom with clothes. Hung on rails, draped over chairs and hung from giant poles across the ceiling. There must have been at least a thousand items of clothing laid out around the room.

A kind lady told them to choose whatever they wanted from the selection. They were told to select enough clothes for two weeks and were all given a different style of large suitcase to put them all in.

Billy chose eight pairs of trousers, three pairs of shoes (two pairs of trainers and one school pair), twelve t-shirts, two hoodies, four jumpers and had a Finian's school uniform, literally made to measure around him, by two gentlemen holding handfuls of tape measures and pins. They were real-life, walking, talking pin cushions.

As he was leaving the room, he realised he'd forgotten to pack any underwear. He dashed back in and stuffed it into the top of his large suitcase, already brimming with new clothes.

That would have been embarrassing thought one of the tailors, putting down his safety pins and wandering over to the sewing machine with Billy's new school blazer.

Billy smiled and looked over to him 'VERY embarrassing,' he said out loud. The tailor nodded his head and then dabbed his sweaty eyebrow with his sleeve.

'Do we get to keep the clothes?' asked Poppy.

'Of course,' said the Prime Minister.

They were all handed black panic devices by the Prime Minister. It looked like a mobile phone screen and was about the same size and weight as a library card.

The Prime Minister spoke in a clear and quiet voice as he offered the instructions. 'Tapping the four corners of the device in any order, provides you with an instant audio link to us here. This is so that we can monitor the situation and provide support to you in an emergency. There are government people staying in places extremely close to the school grounds. We've timed it and they can be on the school grounds to support you within three minutes, whatever time day or night. Rest assured, these experts will be sleeping in their clothes – just in case.'

He pointed out that only in an absolute emergency, would a government person turn up at the school, as if they did their entire mission would end and the young people could no longer gather evidence on the Government's behalf.

'When are we going?' Gracie asked.

The Prime Minister looked down at his watch. 'We're sending Billy first in about forty-five minutes,' he said.

Billy heard his name and looked up in a panic. At first, he thought he'd wet himself. When he looked down, he'd tipped half of his glass of lemonade down his trousers.

'Why me?' he said in a panic.

'Because, two days of preparation have gone into this Billy and you're first on the list. Someone will come with you in the car to make sure you've got your back story absolutely sorted.'

'Do we keep our real names?' Freddie asked.

'Yes, we've done a great deal of research into this.' the PM said confidently. 'None of you have any connections with the school whatsoever, so it's the safest thing to do. Now you all know each other, there's more chance of one of you getting the names wrong as you get used to the place. Our advisors have told us that keeping your names are fine.'

The forty-five minutes passed in what seemed like forty-five seconds and before he knew it, Billy was back in the car again. His suitcase was in the boot behind him and a lady with an incredibly bad haircut sat next to him. It was parted in the middle, with weird tufts at the back – like it had not been brushed for the past twenty years. She did have a reassuring voice though, which made Billy feel a little less like the snakes in his stomach would burst out of his belly button and nibble on the weird tufts of hair at the back of her head.

EIGHTEEN

He had gone over his story a million times with Mrs WeirdHair. The more he went over it, the more he kept getting it wrong. Where he's come from, what his lifestyle is like, the previous schools he'd been to. It was just all becoming a bit of a blur.

The government car drove down some very narrow country lanes, only just avoiding several foxes and badgers scavenging for food at the side of the road.

Mrs Tuftattheback felt it necessary to give Billy a running commentary on the time remaining on the journey.

'Approximately fourteen minutes to go now Billy,' she would say. Two minutes later she added, 'Approximately twelve and a half minutes now Billy. How are you feeling?'

Billy wanted to say, 'The same as I felt two minutes ago,' but felt this was a little rude and would only just about be allowed by his Mum and Dad at the best of times.

Eventually, the car slowed right down as it approached a very grand looking driveway. There were trees that seemed like they were exactly equal distance apart and looked like they were the same height. Around about the size of a house. Billy thought they must have been planted many years ago and were grown in perfect unison.

Mr and Mrs Scratchnsiff could never manage anything like that, Billy thought.

My husband could never maintain trees like that, thought Mrs Hairpiece.

'I'm sure he could if you asked,' Billy said out loud, smiling at her.

'Oh yes, your special thing, I forgot about that.' Mrs Tufty nervously put her hand up to her head and tugged what looked like a bit of cornflake from a matted bit in the back of her head. She studied it. Billy thought she was considering putting it in her mouth and as his breakfast came back up into his throat, he was very pleased that she did not.

As the car came to a stop, a very angry looking gentleman came quickly out of two huge wooden doors. The doors looked like they had taken about twenty years to make and in the centre was carved a huge crest. Billy instantly recognised it from the top of the school letter in the Prime Minister's office. They'd been given a pack of things to familiarise themselves with and a map of the school so that they could learn roughly what was where before they arrived.

The angry gentleman was wearing a black cape draped around his arms.

'He can't have just finished at university,' Billy said, remembering the boring graduation ceremony he'd had to go to a few years ago when his Aunty Hannah finished her degree.

'No, Billy. He's the Headmaster.' said Mrs Hairytufts. 'This was unexpected.'

She looked directly at him. 'I'm really sorry to do this Billy, but I'm going to have to pretend I'm your mother, it's the only way we're going to get around this.'

Mr Crinklebottom, who Billy now recognised as the

Headmaster, from the photo they'd been given in their pack, let out a huge fake smile as he walked towards the car. He seemed very grand and his suit made him look like he was one hundred and ninety. He looked to see which side of the car Billy was on and then walked around and opened the door.

'You're here early young man. Welcome to Finian's.' Mr Crinklebottom said.

Immediately after he spoke, he let out a short, sharp fart. It was the sort of fart that old people do without thinking sometimes. Billy tried his best not to laugh. He looked around at Mrs Tufty to check she'd heard and noticed that she had removed a tissue and was pretending to cry.

Through fake tears and really bad acting she started saying through a series of sniffs, 'Oh, my boy. I can't believe I have to leave you here. I just can't believe it.'

Billy stared at her with wide eyes, not believing that he was going to have to play along with this rubbish.

'Don't worry mother,' he said in the poshest voice he could manage, 'I'll be fine.'

He stepped out of the car and shook the awaiting hand of Mr Crinklebottom. His hands felt old and wrinkly and his handshake was so firm that Billy thought he was going to try and pull his arm off.

The government driver had already taken Billy's suitcase out of the boot and Billy followed Mr Crinklebottom through the maze of grand corridors with large oil paintings on the wall, until eventually, he was sat down in a green leather chair in Mr Crinklebottom's office.

NINETEEN

'How do you take your tea Billy?' Mr Crinklebottom said, peering up from the documents that Billy had brought with him and the forms that Billy had been asked to fill in by the Prime Minister.

Billy thought to himself nervously, hang on, we weren't told how to react to this?

He hated hot drinks. A few years earlier, he had tried coffee, with sugar Dad had added to make it sweet, and still spat out the entire mouthful, infecting the entire sugar bowl with his coffee and spit. Dad was furious that he had ruined the entire bowl and Billy had not touched a drop of tea or coffee since.

'White with one sugar, please' he said to Mr Crinklebottom – clearing his throat halfway through the sentence because he was so nervous. He had remembered back to what Dad said to Grandma every weekend when they visited her little retirement flat. Dad always had to remind Grandma how he took his tea. Each time, Grandma would appear with two mugs saying, 'I didn't add any sugar Sonny because I couldn't remember what you said.' Every week, Billy had to watch Dad awkwardly sip sugarless tea, pretending he was enjoying it in front of his Mum.

Mr Crinklebottom picked up the telephone and pressed a button.

'Two teas and bring the honey in. Thank you.' He barked at the person on the other end of the phone like an old dog, very impolite and rude. Billy vowed to himself in that very moment, that whatever he did in the future – if his boss was like him, he would quit the job immediately.

Mr Crinklebottom stared at the papers intently and Billy stared down at his shoes. Even though he was pleased with the new clothes, he still felt uncomfortable in them, like the way you would if someone gave you a million pounds tomorrow morning. It wouldn't be a bad feeling, but what would you do first?

Instead of running through his story again in his head, Billy decided on five reasons why he now hated Mr Crinklebottom:

He farted without knowing
His voice sounded like the next door neighbour's annoying dog
He wore a cape like it was his graduation day
His office smelt of mouldy cheese and burnt wood
He was about to quiz him on a life that he'd learnt just a few hours ago

What can I say to really test this lad and show him how powerful I am, thought Mr Crinklebottom.

Billy could barely disguise how disgusted he was with the thought he had just heard.

'So Billy,' Mr Crinklebottom spoke out loud with the same fake smile, 'what do you think you'll enjoy most about Finian's?'

'Well, I think...sir... I'll enjoy the cross-country. I'm part of a running club at the weeken-

'Indeed,' Crinklebottom interrupted instantly, 'we have the finest runners the county has to offer. We've won the county cup for twenty years in a row.'

Billy didn't know what to say. He obviously hated cross-country running and hoped with every morsel of his being that he would not be at the school long enough to have to take part in a race.

'What's your favourite subject at school Billy?'

'Erm...well...' Billy pondered.

At that moment, the door burst open and a young, pretty lady walked in with flowers on her dress, carrying a tray. She smiled at Billy. It was a warm smile, not fake like Crinklebottom's. She had lovely flowing ginger hair that looked like tiny pieces of silk and her face sparkled in the light through the tiny window in the corner.

'On the table please,' Mr Crinklebottom said sternly. 'How I wish you would love me the way I am in love with you.'

Billy let out a snort and looked up at Mr Crinklebottom. Had he said that or thought that?

'Here you are, Headmaster.' the pretty lady said.

'Yes, yes, come along, come along.' Crinklebottom replied.

Miss Flowersondress set the tray down hurriedly and started panicking that she was not moving fast enough.

'I'm mean to you because I love you. I LOVE YOU WITH ALL MY HEART.'

This time, Billy was staring at Crinklebottom directly, there was no doubt that his lips were not moving and he was hearing his thoughts. But, when he shouted 'I LOVE YOU' Billy started smiling. Crinklebottom's brain sang the last four words 'WITH ALL MY HEART'. It sounded like the sort of tacky love ballad that Dave Simpson played on the radio every morning at 8am just before he left for school. Billy started giggling and had to pinch his arm.

'Something funny boy?' Crinklebottom said.

'No, sir. Sorry.'

Instead of returning to the conversation, Crinklebottom distracted himself by bragging about the school some more, including taking Billy through the fourteen types of tea that he has instant access to. Billy thought to himself if I ever do have a million pounds, I would never send my child to a school that cares more about fourteen types of tea than they do welcoming new kids.

'Seems strange,' Crinklebottom barked, 'why on earth would your parents change schools midterm? Do they not care about your education?'

'Er, well...' Billy replied, remembering his story to the letter, 'my father changed jobs you see, so we had to.'

'Was it not a boarding school?'

This was a snag, the Prime Minister had not thought in this amount of detail.

'Well, yes, it was a boarding school sir.'

'So why couldn't you stay there until the end of the summer term? Start afresh in September?'

'Well...erm, Mum and Dad wanted me close by...for weekend outings and things.'

'Our children don't leave the school at weekends, they stay here with us Billy.' Crinklebottom replied.

He adjusted his glasses and peered over them, leaning forward slightly, Billy heard his inner voice bellow 'Something about this doesn't add up, this boy is lying to me.'

'I know...I know it seems unusual,' Billy said, growing

in confidence, 'but Mum and Dad wanted to do it all in one go, the job, the school. It means we could enjoy our summer holiday with everything sorted.'

'Very well,' Crinklebottom barked back at him.

Billy then heard Mr Crinklebottom think, I want him to tell me that he knows about this school and it's where he wants to be or else he will NOT BE TRUSTWORTHY.

'To be honest sir...' Billy said, 'Finian's Field Manor is the only school I've ever wanted to come to. I've wanted to be here since I was a little boy. I love the history and that it was opened in 1562 with only four pupils. I love everything you've brought to the school as the Headmaster in the last twenty years and I can't wait to be part of it.'

Mr Crinklebottom looked at him with furrowed eyebrows. All of the lines on his forehead seemed to soften a little bit.

'I think you'll be very happy here' Crinklebottom said. 'One of the prefects will be along shortly to show you to your dormitory. In the meantime, if you have any questions you can ask away. My door is never open, but you can ask one of the other pupils or teachers. Off you go.'

That was it, he had made it through the first round. It felt like X Factor or Britain's Got Talent. He wanted to leap up into the air and shout, 'I've made the live final!' but he managed to resist the temptation.

As he stood up to leave and approached the old dog's grand office door, he heard his voice bellow out at him. The only trouble with this superpower was you had to look at the person talking to check whether they were actually saying the words, or whether they were simply thinking them. This time, Crinklebottom was speaking to him in a very quiet and evil tone.

'We're on the cusp of something great here, Billy. No

doubt you'll hear about it all over the coming days and weeks. Suffice it to say, your parents made the right choice in sending you here. In just a few weeks' time, the whole world will know what it is to be part of Finian's.'

Then the serious tone subsided and he added a little more warmly, 'I hope you'll feel very part of it all here.'

Billy gave a half smile and managed to say 'thank you' as he walked out of the room and plonked himself on the large musty green sofa outside the old dog's office.

TWENTY

Finian's was not a difficult place to like. If it were not for the strict teachers and the fact that nobody seemed to speak to each other, Billy would have quite liked it here.

It was like a grand hotel with swimming pools, libraries, huge fountains in the garden and peacocks wandering around the grounds like it was just normal.

The entrance hall was so vast, it was the same size as Billy's school hall where they crammed everybody in for their weekly assembly.

The assembly hall was equally ginormous. When you saw somebody on the other side of the room, it was like watching footballers on the pitch from the back of your local stadium.

Even though it was a dormitory and six boys or girls shared a room, each section had an incredibly large bed, a television that came down from the ceiling on a high-tech pully system, a wardrobe and a chest of drawers on either side of each bed.

'I don't have to share with anyone else, do I?' Billy asked the prefect, who had shown him to his dorm.

'The bed's yours' the posh older boy said, 'but there's six others in every room, including a prefect.'

Billy could not believe it. His section of the dormitory was four times larger than his bedroom at home. Billy thought it must cost hundreds of thousands of pounds to send your child here. He nearly asked the prefect what the fees were, but then remembered it could blow his cover.

'Any questions?' the prefect asked.

Billy thought for a second. He wanted to ask something important. What was the most important thing he could possibly think of in this important moment?

'How do we hear the TV if we're all watching different things at the same time?'

'There's a pair of noise cancelling headphones in your top left-hand drawer' the prefect replied. 'TV time is for an hour between seven and eight pm. You must make sure the headphones are placed back in the drawer, if not they won't charge for the following day. Any more questions?'

'Erm...No, that's all,' Billy said.

'Assembly is at 8:30am. Except on Saturday when it's 9am.'

'You have assembly on Saturday?' Billy asked nervously.

'We have lessons on Saturday morning, sports throughout Saturday afternoon.'

Billy could not believe what he was hearing. Saturday was for staying in your pyjamas, eating biscuits on the sofa, stealing chocolate from Mum's secret stash and playing computer games with Dad. School on a Saturday was the worst idea he had ever heard of.

'Well, if there's no further questions, I'll be off. If you need me, you can use that panel on the wall. Press call and 1213, it will bleep my watch and I'll come straight up.' With that, the prefect disappeared.

Billy had chosen not to hear his thoughts, he couldn't face hearing what the posh older boy thought of him, he would rather not know.

All of a sudden, he heard a huge whirring noise. As it got louder, Billy was afraid that the roof was going to fall in. Just as he had prepared to dash immediately out of the dormitory and down the stone stairs, he saw the bottom of a helicopter coming into view. It slowly came into land on the field outside the dormitory. Once the blades had stopped rotating and the engine had been switched off, he saw Gracie hop out of the helicopter with a huge smile on her face.

He felt relieved to see his new friend, knowing that he was no longer here alone.

He rushed over to the window and started frantically waving at her. She glanced upwards and spotted Billy and gave a gentle wave back at him, which she disguised by flicking her fringe with the tips of her fingers.

The window Billy was stood at, was locked in four different places with heavy bolts. Considering the glass was so old and flimsy looking, four bolts seemed a bit ridiculous. Billy opened each one in turn. They were completely stiff, like they had not been opened for the last fifty years.

As he prized the window open, he just managed to call Gracie's name before she disappeared out of view through the main entrance. She looked at him in a horrified way, knowing that they were never supposed to have met before.

Billy shouted down in a half whisper, 'The Head Teacher, he's going to try and catch you out. Answer all the questions and try and talk about tea.'

Gracie did not know what on earth he was going on about and looked at him, mouthing 'WHAT?'

'TALK ABOUT TEABAGS!' Billy shout-whispered.

Gracie's face looked like Billy was speaking to her in Japanese, she was so confused.

At that moment, she looked straight ahead and almost jumped out of her skin. Then the creepy cape of Mr Crinklebottom appeared in view and he offered Gracie a wrinkly handshake and the fake smile that Billy had seen before.

Gracie disappeared out of view and Billy thought to himself, 'You're on your own now. Good luck Gracie.'

As Billy turned around from the window, he noticed a large wooden flap on the door. He walked over to it and it opened quite easily. Inside was a tiny, metal, four-sided room. Billy had absolutely no idea what it was. As he started peering inside and inspecting the tiny metal walls, he heard footsteps coming along the corridor. Not wanting to get told off within an hour of being in the building, he leapt inside. He felt as claustrophobic as he had in his airing cupboard at home, when he was hiding from his Dad on the toilet.

As he turned around, he brought his knees up to his chest to give himself more space and quickly shut the white wooden flap.

Why on earth did I go in here? Billy thought to himself, I could have easily been just checking it out, I wouldn't have got into trouble for doing that surely?

But it was too late, there he was, sitting completely guilty in the small metal case in the wall.

It was not one person arriving in the room but two. They were both ladies' voices he could hear. One was telling the other about getting her toenails clipped at the weekend because her ingrowing toenails were getting unbearably painful. All the toenail talk was making Billy want to be sick. He imagined this particular lady to have mould growing all over her toes, smelling like the old Christmas cheese that Dad insisted on buying every year at the supermarket.

After a few minutes, without warning, the white flap flew open and a whole heap of white sheets were thrown onto Billy. Neither of the ladies looked in there. The sheets stank of smelly teenager and expensive body spray.

Billy moved the sheets off his face and breathed in a breath of fresher air, as quietly as he could, wondering to himself how he was going to explain the situation to Mouldy Foot and her mate.

He need not have worried. The white flap closed again and Billy sat there in the pitch black.

All of a sudden, Billy felt the metal case move. There was a loud whirring sound and Billy felt the floor feel like it was giving way beneath him. He was travelling downwards at quite a speed and could not work out whether he was falling, or still inside the metal case.

Without warning, the case stopped and Billy was thrown upwards. Billy checked he was still alive and felt a sense of relief that he had made it in one piece. Just when his heart had returned to a slightly more normal rhythm, the metal box began to tip upwards on a diagonal. Billy took a deep breath, certain that this was the moment he was going to die. His final thought in his life was going to be that he'd let the Prime Minister and all the others down.

This time Billy really was falling, but not very far. After tumbling through the air, headfirst, he landed on the largest pile of dirty washing he had ever seen.

As he looked around, it was like he was in the middle of a cave. There were seven or eight huge washing machines and drips coming from the ceiling. Huge boxes of washing powder were all over the place, with remnants of the white powder on the damp and dusty floor.

On the right-hand side, there were pristinely folded piles

of clean washing.

Ah well, Billy thought, that's one way of finding the utility room.

He picked himself up off the floor, dusting off his knees and walked through a maze of corridors covered in pipes running down the walls. He walked past a boiler that was bigger than his kitchen at home. As he approached the doorway into the main school corridor, he could hear two people talking just outside the door.

He could make out two faces through the small crack in the door. Thinking through all of the faces they had been shown in their pack in the Prime Minister's office, he worked out it was the two Deputy Head Teachers. He put his right ear to the crack in the doorway, to try and tune in to their conversation.

TWENTY-ONE

'Six new pupils, at this time of year,' said the one that looked like she smelt of rotten cabbage.

'And so close to next Thursday as well,' replied the stern looking man with dandruff in his eyebrows.

'I've told him exactly what I thought of it…exactly…' said Cabbagefeatures.

'And what did he say?' said Dandrufftufts.

'I'll tell you exactly what he said… he said I shouldn't be meddling in things that don't concern me.'

'That's perfectly outrageous.'

'Well,' replied Cabbagemouth, 'it may well be outrageous, but it certainly wasn't perfect.'

'It can't come a moment sooner,' said Eyebrows, 'my wife and I have been looking at private yachts and country cottages. She's got her eye set on one.'

'How much?' said Cabbage.

'Half a million pounds,' Tuftybrows replied, bringing his index finger up to his eyebrow, scratching it a little and then pinching the tiny molecules of hair dust onto the floor.

'I just can't believe Philip was brave enough to send the latest codes by email. I said to him "Mr Crankbottom…"'

At that moment, Billy saw the flash of a black cape come into view followed by an elongated 'yes...?' from a booming, deep voice that he recognised.

Mr Crankbottom had clearly appeared in the doorway and the two Deputy Heads had sprung to attention as if Crankbottom were the head of the army.

'Ah. Good morning Headmaster' said Mrs Cabbagebreath, 'jolly good show sending the latest code by email.'

'Splendiforous,' added Mr Tuftybrows, 'absolute genius. Couldn't have done any better myself.'

'Some staff felt it was rather brave to send something out so...well, erm...publicly.', replied Mrs Cabbagebreath.

'There was nothing public about it at all,' Crankbottom snapped. 'FoxgloveNorth242left' is useless without the other two codes, even if it had leaked out, nobody in their right mind is going to be able to work out what it is. I'll see you at assembly.'

Billy saw the black of his cape swoosh around the door and Crankbottom disappeared from his restricted view. Then, just when he thought the coast was clear, he heard the footsteps stop.

'I've been meaning to ask actually...' came Crankbottom's inquisitive sounding voice a little in the distance.

'What is it?' said Cabbage and Tufty, almost in unison, like he was some sort of Greek god that they were about to bow down to.

'When I walk quickly around the school...' Crankbottom said, sounding a little nervous.

'Yes?' said Cabbage.

'When I quickly walk around the school, does my black cape swoosh out to the side?'

'I beg your pardon Headmaster?' said Tuftybrows.

'When I walk the corridors of the school that I'm proud to be Headmaster in and I turn a corner or move to the side, does my father's black cape swoosh sideways like I'm very important...here, I'll show you.'

Billy heard some footsteps and a bit of kerfuffle, but he could not make out what was going on through the crack in the door.

'Well...' Crankbottom said. 'Does it?'

'Erm...not really Headmaster' said Cabbagepits.

'Oh, dang and blast...hold on.'

Billy heard a few more footsteps before Crankbottom said 'How about now?'

'Erm...well yes, I suppose it did flail a little out to the side that time Headmaster' Tuftybrows said.

'Excellent' came the booming voice of Crankbottom before his footsteps grew more distant.

Billy was certain he must have gone this time.

'That man, has far too much time on his hands' said Cabbage.

'He's very welcome to come and teach a few of my classes.' replied Mr Brows.

'Well, just a few weeks longer. I'm sure we can hold out for an early retirement until then.'

The conversation grew quieter as the two were clearly walking away. Billy turned around and slid down some of the metal pipes on the wall, so that he was sitting on the floor. His memory had always been 'just fine.' He could remember simple facts and figures, but knew he was going to have to get so much better being part of a group like this.

What was the information he needed to remember?

The two Deputy Heads were named Cabbage Features and Tufty Eyebrows – NO.

Mr Crankbottom was trying to make his cape swoosh in the corridor? – NO.
The Deputy Heads were set to be retired in two weeks – YES and
FoxgloveNorth242Left – YES.

Billy sat up and said the last phrase over and over. FoxGloveNorth242Left. Fox-Glove-North-2-4-2-Left. What did it mean? It was the sort of clue he did not ever feel he would be able to work out. He suddenly sighed and had an absolute crisis of confidence being part of this new group. Part of him wished more than anything that he was in the car with Dad on the way to school, getting nagged by Mum to brush his teeth or just, doing normal things. This was such a big deal all of a sudden, his chest started to feel a little tight and then the Prime Minister flashed into his head and he took another deep breath in. He was going to be alright.

He tentatively pushed the door and it let out the most enormous creak. The sound was like how you imagine an old man would fart at a wedding at an inappropriate time, just before the couple said 'I do.' It seemed to go on forever. The corridor was empty, so Billy shut the door again and noticed that the doorway was not really a doorway at all. The door seemed to click into place and formed part of the wall again. There's a secret corridor that might come in useful, he thought to himself as he wandered down the corridor.

As he came around the corner, he noticed the large assembly hall, filled to the rafters with hundreds of people from floor to ceiling. Although the seating was clearly tiered like a football stadium, Billy couldn't believe how many there were. Great, he thought to himself, my first day and I'm late for assembly.

TWENTY-TWO

At last, some good news. Billy was not told off for being late for assembly, in fact, nobody seemed to notice. More good news, their plan appeared to have worked so far. The school and, more importantly, Mr Crankbottom seemed to have no idea whatsoever that the six young people were connected to one another. The final bit of good news? Because they were all new, they'd been sat together at lunch.

There were no trays, the cutlery was gold and the food was presented in large, what looked like, plastic containers. It was not see-through like a normal sort of lunchbox, but sort of light-wood coloured. The lasagne was actually really tasty, full of vegetables – one of which was purple and Billy had never seen it before.

'What the hell is this?' Max asked lifting up the stringy purple thing on his golden fork and pulling a face that looked like someone had strangled his goldfish in front of him.

'That's aubergine, Max,' said Gracie with a smile on her face.

'Auber-what?' Max replied.

'It looks like a giant purple kidney bean.' said Poppy.

'What's a kidney bean?' Max asked.

'Have you never eaten any vegetables?' asked Freddie.

'I'm more of a sausage and waffle kind of guy,' Max replied, with a small bit of aubergine hanging out of his mouth. 'Urgh. It tastes like a rotten dead duck...'

'What does a dead duck taste like?' Billy asked, adding 'actually don't answer that.'

Mrs Berry, the school canteen lady, looked like a berry. It was almost as if her parents had realised that her surname was Berry when she was a child, so did everything in their power to make her look like a berry. She had flush red cheeks that spread up to her eyes and down towards her chin and her tummy poked through her stretchy, red cardigan. Her hair was clearly dyed brown, as there were grey bits poking out of the roots and she had a scrunchy holding it all up in the middle like...the top of a berry.

She was walking around the room and stacking the food packaging up piece by piece. After she had collected four or five of them, she walked over to a small metal container and threw them all in.

Every few minutes, a very tall and thin man would appear, with a wooden mallet in one hand. His face was rather pink and blotchy too. In fact, he looked like the sort of pencil you would find in your pencil case. He was so thin and frail looking, it was as if you would pick him up and he would crumble into pieces. Alternatively, you could just turn him upside down and rub out the wrong answer to your maths question. He was clearly the caretaker, as he wore a dark grey overcoat and across the back, somebody had badly sewn in 'Mr Watson, Caretaker' with light blue thread.

Mr Watson would pick up the metal container and empty the contents into a pile outside. He looked over them all, lovingly like they were baby chicks that had just hatched.

'Why's he looking at everybody's leftover lunch containers like he's in love with them?' Freddie asked.

'I was just wondering the same thing,' said Gracie.

Mr Watson's smile turned into the angriest frown and his cheeks flushed crimson like he had sucked a red-hot chilli. It was as if all of the baby chicks he was admiring had turned into huge hairy spiders. Without warning, he raised the wooden mallet above his head and brought it down with an enormous wallop.

The packaging exploded into tiny pieces, bits flying up everywhere and back down onto the patio.

'Well, that was barbaric and unnecessary.' said Poppy.

'Ah,' said Max, 'so now, they're going to feed that to the animals.'

Sure enough, Mr Watson collected the larger pieces into a big pile and carried them over to the base of the field, where there were a large number of cows chewing on the grass. He dropped them into the metal container. One by one, the cows meandered over towards it and started chewing the packaging.

'That is going to change the world,' Freddie whispered. 'The Prime Minister is right.'

'That's what Mr Watson just thought,' Billy said, I heard him thinking it.

'So, this is a bit weird,' Gracie said, 'what do we do now?'

'I was just thinking the same thing' Max said, 'we've got less than a week.'

Billy had told the others about the conversation he had heard that morning. Whilst he was trying to remember the code word he also thought back to what he heard CabbagePits and TuftyEyes say right at the beginning. As his eyes scoured around the dinner hall and he saw Tufty rubbing his head and thousands of dandruff pieces fall over his lasagne like parmesan cheese, he remembered.

'Next Thursday,' Billy announced proudly.

'That was a bit random,' Freddie said back.

'We've got less than a week. It's Friday today, Saturday tomorrow. Them two over there,' he pointed subtly at Cabbage and Eyebrows, 'they said it was weird that five new pupils joined so close to next Thursday. That must be their press conference day.'

'We'd better let the PM know,' said Poppy.

At that moment, Billy saw the distinct black cloak of Crinklebottom walking down the corridor. He was deliberately stopping and looking to see if his cape was flailing out to the side, just as he wished it had been earlier that day.

Billy focused in on him intently, he heard his thoughts repeating the phrase, Friday briefing, Friday briefing, Friday briefing.

'He's thinking Friday briefing,' Billy said to the others.

'Friday what?' Max asked.

'Of course, the Prime Minister said they have a staff briefing on a Friday afternoon, they're bound to announce things there.' Gracie declared.

'Makes sense for Freddie to go this afternoon, as he can be there without them knowing,' Poppy said.

'Definitely,' Freddie said, 'I'm happy to.'

'It would be good if Billy and Poppy could be there too.' Gracie said.

Billy's heart sank. He had been hoping for a lazy afternoon trying to make sense of all of this.

'I've noticed that the air conditioning units are massive and they're everywhere' Gracie added. 'There's bound to be enough room to crawl along. All you have to do is find where there's a way in and then find your way to above the staff room.'

'Why me?' Poppy asked.

'Because some of them might talk in different languages and even if they don't, Billy can hear what they're thinking. We need to find out what time the briefing is.'

Mrs Berry was still sauntering around looking like a berry. Every so often she would do a half-burp-half-hiccup and she would move her hand up to her chin to brush off the bit of saliva that had dripped from her bottom lip. When she got closer to the table, Max turned to her.

'Excuse me Mrs Gooseberry, I mean Mrs Berry...'

'Yes dear?'

'Erm...we're new here and we don't know what happens now on a Friday afternoon.' Max said.

Mrs Berry leant down towards the table. Her berry coloured top creaked and strained as if the buttons were ready to pop off. She spoke in a whisper, like she was telling the five superheroes the biggest secret they had ever heard.

'Friday, is physical education. The teachers have their Friday briefing in the staff room at three pm before they go to the pub. Now, as it's your first few days here, you could always say you have a slight cold and have a little nap instead...'

She smiled like she had predicted the winning lottery numbers and written them all a cheque for millions of pounds, then she tapped her bright red nose and walked off, wiping more spit from her bottom lip.

TWENTY-THREE

The plan was set in place. Freddie would be invisible, waiting outside the staff room door and follow the last member of staff into the room before the door was closed. He would have his mobile device on him and would play this back to Max and Gracie in the girls' dormitory.

Billy and Poppy would have to figure out where the air conditioning unit was and try and find a way up and over to the staff room.

The tubes at the top of the ceilings reminded Billy of a water park. They snaked in all different directions and looked like they were wrapped in tin foil. Every five metres or so, the tin-foiled-tubes pointed downwards to a huge vent in the middle. They looked like you could fit a person through them, but Billy was not sure.

Poppy and Billy carefully followed the foil tubes out of the hall and along the corridor.

They look like they've got a lot smaller in here, Poppy thought to herself.

Billy looked at her and said 'I was just thinking the same.'

Poppy smiled and then thought about the time her little brother was so desperate for the toilet, he went in a wheelbarrow in the garden. Billy turned to her with a look of horror.

'That'll teach you for seeing my thoughts, Billy.'

'Why would you do that to me?' Billy said.

The silver tubes fell down the wall to what looked like a huge store cupboard. Poppy and Billy checked there was nobody else in the corridor, moved the silver spoon holding the catch in place and opened the creaky door.

The room sounded like an old steam engine. There was a buzz like thirty ancient fridges stacked on top of each other and the buzz rang around Billy's head, it was the worst noise ever.

'It's going to be absolutely freezing' Poppy said.

'I don't think it's on, even though it sounds like it is,' Billy replied, 'it was so hot in that dinner hall.'

Sure enough, there did not seem to be any cold air coming out of the vent next to the machine. The machine itself looked more like the cockpit of an aeroplane, filled with dials and pressure gauges of all different sizes. The numbers went from one to ten and on each of them, the pointer was set at one. There was a bright blue LED light above each of them. Although the machine was very old, it looked reliable and robust and neither Billy nor Poppy felt particularly nervous.

'It looks like the sort of robot that could take over the world,' Poppy said.

'I think so too,' Billy replied.

'I think we need something to pull this vent off,' Poppy said.

'What, like a stronger person?'

'I think we could probably get away with a screwdriver.'

'Oh, I'll just grab the screwdriver out of my trousers that I carry around with me,' Billy said sarcastically.

'Don't be rude, Billy.'

They both smiled at each other and wondered what to do next. Poppy's eyes lit up and she quickly opened the door and grabbed the silver spoon from inside the lock. She started trying to pull the vent off using the end of the spoon but the top of the handle was bending further and further out of place.

'What about the spoon end?' Billy said, 'Here, give it to me.'

Billy turned the spoon and slid it underneath the vent. Like he was spooning jelly out of a bowl, he pushed and pulled on the handle. The metal bent a little but did not move.

Try the corners for goodness sake, Poppy thought to herself.

Billy looked at her. 'Alright clever clogs,' he said to her with a smile.

Almost as soon as he slid the spoon over to the corner, the piece of metal flew off of the vent and onto the floor. It was like a slow motion sequence in a film and clanged on the floor for what seemed like five minutes. The sound was louder than a rock concert.

The hole was at least three-foot-wide and both of them stuck their heads up and peered into the pitch-black tube.

They were both thinking the same thing, how the hell were they going to climb up there?

'You see those bolts sticking out up the side?' Poppy pointed out, 'We'll have to use those.'

'That would be perfect,' Billy said, 'if we were cats or squirrels.'

'We'll just have to do our best Billy. Come on, I'll go first.'

Poppy climbed into the tube and sat on the metal rim. Suddenly, Billy heard footsteps in the corridor.

'Someone's coming,' Billy said in a panic.

'Don't worry, they won't come in here,' Poppy whispered back, 'climb in here just in case.'

Billy climbed inside the metal tube and placed his feet on the metal rim.

The door swung open and light poured up the tube through the open doorway.

Someone was pottering around the room muttering about missing spoons and the fact that the vent cover had fallen off. The two of them heard the clang as the person lifted the vent off the floor. It screeched like a cat's claws on a blackboard. The person, whoever it was, placed the vent cover back into place and punched the sides of it back into place. It was such a heavy set of fist pumps that it caused Billy and Poppy to lightly hop into the air and back down again. Poppy put her finger in her mouth and bit down hard to stop herself from screaming.

Then the footsteps left the store cupboard and the door closed, sharply. The person slid something else, instead of a spoon across the catch and the lock to secure the door.

'He's locked the door Poppy,' Billy said.

'We'll be fine, don't worry.' she replied.

Poppy and Billy looked upwards again into the darkness and Poppy stood up and put her left foot onto the first bolt. Like a spider she slowly manoeuvred her way up from bolt to bolt until Billy could not see her anymore.

'Are you up?' Billy asked.

'Yeah, I've reached the flat bit.'

Billy put his left foot on the first bolt and instantly his foot slipped back down onto the metal ledge, causing another loud clang.

'I can't do it' Billy called up to her.

'Oh just get on with it Billy!' Poppy shouted back and it

echoed around the tinfoil chamber into Billy's ears. Eventually, unlike the graceful spider that Poppy had become, Billy slid up the silver slide like a lizard with a missing leg.

A few metres later he was at the same level as Poppy, at the top on the flat level.

'That's got to be the worst bit over.' Poppy said.

The two of them crawled along the top of the tube, dodging various vents with a sheer vertical drop.

'Be careful,' Billy said, 'if we fall down there, we'll drop straight into the room underneath.'

Eventually, the two of them saw a flurry of movement underneath one of the sheer drops and Billy saw the flash of Crinklebottom's coat.

'Look,' he said to Poppy.

'Yes, I can see him,' she replied, adding 'we need to get down to that small metal platform.'

'What if it doesn't take our weight?' Billy said.

Poppy looked at him nervously and then moved her legs over the gap, lowering her body down gently onto the platform. She slowly lowered her weight onto it. There was a slight creak, but nobody in the staff room below appeared to notice, the same flurry of movement continued.

'That'll never take me as well' Billy whispered, 'and I need to see them to be able to hear what they're thinking.'

'Give it a go,' Poppy replied, 'just be careful.'

Like Poppy had, Billy lowered his legs over the edge and slowly lowered himself down. As he transferred his weight from his arms to his legs, the metal ledge bent downwards slightly with a fairly loud creak. Then it stopped. Billy and Poppy both shut their eyes, certain they were about to fall through the vent into the room below, but it seemed to hold them.

'Now don't move.' Poppy whispered.

'I really hope that Freddie is in there and this isn't a complete waste of time,' Billy replied.

TWENTY-FOUR

Luckily, Crinklebottom's staff address was directly below the air vent. Billy could see a clear line of him through the cracks in the metal.

This was not like any other staff room. Strange as it is to believe, only five things are certain in staff rooms around the world:

They stink of coffee.
They have teachers moaning in them.
The teachers talk most often about kids that they HATE.
The room is filled with boring books that are at least twenty years old.
Someone, somewhere, will be marking a piece of work and giving some poor person an 'F.'

This staff room had a snooker table, a vending machine, a hot tub, a state-of-the-art coffee machine, mood lighting, lovely oak furniture and four massive, comfortable sofas.

If you thought that Mrs Berry looked much like a berry in the lunch hall, she really looked like a berry in the hot tub wearing her disgusting red swimming costume, with her belly poking out of the water with bubbles rippling all around her. She'd even put redberry coloured lipstick on. The mobile phone in her hand? A BlackBerry…obviously.

Mr Crinklebottom stood still and raised his hand in the air. The room fell silent, followed by a quick fart from Crinklebottom's bottom. He pretended he hadn't noticed and carried on regardless. Poppy sniggered and Billy quickly placed his hand over her mouth.

He spoke slowly and spoke in exactly the same way to the other teachers as he did to the students. 'You'll be pleased to know, there is now a template letter of your resignation on the staff download section of the website.' A small scattering of applause followed, with a little cheer from some random people in the corner that Billy and Poppy could not see.

'The time,' he added 'is nearly nigh. By next Wednesday you will all be unemployed, with seven hundred and eighty-six thousand pounds being deposited directly into your bank accounts.'

Another louder scatter of clapping and cheering followed.

'Next Wednesday afternoon all the members of the national press and major television channels will be in our school hall and we will be telling the world about our biofuel recipe and our edible packaging.'

The applause got louder and louder and some teachers were so excited, they were stamping their feet on the floor. The air vent had started to shake and Billy put his hands against the side to steady himself.

'CharlesDickensTale142, FoxgloveNorth242Left and Wallshaveears247 have been three code words that have kept this top secret from the world and I thank each and every one of you for your discretion.'

Poppy looked up at Billy as if this was the most important

Christmas shopping list in the history of the world. Billy nodded back.

'What you may not know,' Crinklebottom added, 'is that I plan to shut the school down entirely. I've had an offer for one of the companies we've partnered with to turn the site into a factory to mass produce this packaging stuff and send it out to the entire world. The students will be redistributed to other nearby schools. Families will not be pleased...but who cares, we'll all be rich.'

The next cheer was so loud that the foil box around Billy and Poppy shook heavily. Billy was so nervous that his mouth had filled with saliva and a small bit of it dripped out and down through the vent, directly onto Crinklebottom's head.

He raised his arm up to his scalp and dabbed at his head. He looked at his fingers containing Billy's spit and then, get this, he actually sniffed it. Then he looked upwards directly at the vent. Poppy and Billy stood, dead still, barely able to breathe. Crinklebottom had a strange look on his face, a combination of sheer anger and rage mixed with confusion.

He barked a command across the room, 'Watson, please sort the air conditioning! It's dripping again.'

Mr Watson, the caretaker, appeared beneath the vent and stared upwards. As Billy moved his body naturally back, trying to disappear from sight, he noticed Freddie crouched behind the hot tub. He stared at Watson who appeared to be looking right back at him through the cracks in the metal.

It feels like there's something up there, but that's impossible. Too cold for rats, Watson was thinking to himself.

The thinnest caretaker in the world took a ceramic bowl from the nearby sink and placed it underneath the vent. What would make the problem go away now? Billy knew that every single person in the room wanted to see a drip fall into the bowl and for the attention to go back to Crinklebottom's announcement. So, he took aim, gathered the spit at the front of his mouth and allowed it to drip down through the vent and land in the bowl.

Sure enough, it worked. Crinklebottom adjusted his position so that he was stood straight in front of it. When he looked down at Poppy she was staring at him with a look of disgust on her face.

That was the most disgusting thing I've ever seen another person do, she thought to herself.

'I'm sorry' Billy whispered.

'So, does anybody have any questions?' Crinklebottom barked like a lion to his herd of cattle, that he could eat alive at any time. Eventually, somebody was brave enough to speak.

'Pardon monsieur,' a voice came from the staffroom crowd.

'Sorry sir,' Poppy whispered up to Billy.

'Yeah I could've guessed that,' Billy whispered back.

'I've heard that in fact you are not retiring, but you're going to be the managing director of this new company…with ze packaging et l'biofuel.' The voice tailed off at the end, like the teacher was scared of asking Crinklebum the question.

'Alas, it's true,' replied Crinklebottom. 'I do intend to stay on and be the managing director of the new company. If any of you want to work, you'll be very welcome. I know Mrs Berry and Mr Watson have already declared an interest in staying on. My wonderful PA, Trudy, will also be staying on.'

Then Billy heard him thinking, because I'm madly in love with her and I want to be her husband.

He put his hand over his mouth to stop himself from laughing.

'So, to conclude. Keep the codes safe, strictly confidential and…what's that noise?'

A buzzing sound was coming from the jacuzzi. Like a loud mobile phone. All of a sudden, two books fell from the shelves and a cup of coffee was knocked over from the side and smashed onto the floor.

There was pandemonium, everybody reacting like they had seen a ghost…which they basically had.

'I think Freddie's device might have gone off,' Poppy whispered to Billy.

Billy nodded at her and they looked nervously below at paper flying through the air and screams coming from the floor below.

TWENTY-FIVE

However nervous Billy had been carefully clambering up the aluminium piping, he sure as hell got down a lot faster. Each movement, including both Poppy and Billy eventually swinging down the last six feet, was masked by the muffled shouting and screams from the teachers and Mr Crinklebottom.

As Billy dusted himself down, covered in dust from head to foot, he turned to Poppy.

'What were they saying? The language teachers? I couldn't hear their thoughts because I couldn't see them.'

'They were saying,' Poppy stood remembering 'library, walled garden and clocktower. At least I think it was clocktower.'

She stood for a second mouthing the words in Spanish and trying to piece the words together.

'Yes,' she confirmed, 'it was clocktower.'

'Well,' Billy replied, 'it looks like that's all we've got to go on.'

All of a sudden, Billy's pocket came alive with short bursts of buzzing and his perfectly fitting school trousers lit up like Blackpool Pleasure Beach on a Summer's evening. It took him a little while to work out what it was.

Finally, he pulled the device from out of his pocket. The same old 'tap to answer' blared out of the middle like the brightest miniature television. He tapped.

'Hi Bill. Thank goodness. I was worried. I've tried Freddie and Gracie and nobody answered.'

The Prime Minister did look more concerned than any of them had ever seen him, although he became more relieved as he was talking.

'Can you talk now?' he added, 'is it safe?'

'Nothing seems to be safe around here,' Poppy replied.

'Is there anybody else around guys?' the PM asked.

'No, we're in a cupboard,' Billy said, 'don't ask.'

'You're looking ever so dusty.'

'As Billy said,' Poppy interjected...don't ask.'

'So, what have you got for us?' the PM gave a sort of half smile, expecting big news.

'We don't really know anything,' Poppy said, 'but we're working on it.'

'The main news,' Billy lowered his voice to a half whisper, 'is that the press conference has been called for next Wednesday.'

'Right,' the PM replied, 'so it's Tuesday for us at the very latest.'

'It's Friday today' Poppy said, looking across at Billy nervously, 'there seems so much to do.'

'And the schedule, is it accurate?' the Prime Minister asked.

'Yes,' Billy said. 'School tomorrow morning, it's games this afternoon which we managed to sneak out of and Sunday off.'

'And do you have anything? Anything at all?'

'Sort of,' Poppy said. 'We have three code words and three

locations; it seems the three of them are linked.'

Poppy and Billy explained to the Prime Minister the code words and the locations that they had heard throughout the course of the day and his facial expression showed he was just as confused as anybody else. They went on to explain that they were going to look for Freddie, whose device had buzzed and set off World War Three in the staff room.

The Prime Minister agreed to phone again the following day and would try his best to do so at 1pm, after lunch had been served and eaten.

After the call was finished, Poppy and Billy had realised that whoever had entered the room, minutes earlier had relocked the door.

'Brilliant,' Poppy sighed sarcastically, 'now we're locked in here.'

Billy stared through the slits in the doors. 'It looks like it's a main corridor, somebody is bound to walk past at some point.'

'Okay mastermind,' she said, 'and how do you plan on explaining why we're both in a store cupboard and the doors are locked. What are you going to say, that you fell in love with the air conditioning unit?'

'We won't need to,' Billy replied with a wry smile. 'Pssssssst. Gracie. Over here.'

Billy and Poppy could hear footsteps edging closer towards the door.

'What on earth are you both doing in there?' Gracie said in a half whisper, half-defiant shout.

'Don't worry about that now,' Billy shout-whispered, 'just let us out.'

Billy and Poppy heard some scuffling by the door and it opened. Gracie gave them a beaming smile, 'we wondered where you'd got to.'

Billy and Poppy looked back at her, exhausted, the sort of look you give your Mum when she's still talking to her friends and all you want to do is get in the car and go home.

Poppy looked at Gracie and asked, 'Is Freddie safe? Is he with you?'

Before Gracie had the opportunity to answer, the distinct voice of Crinklebottom was heard on the other side of the corridor. Billy grabbed Gracie's school blazer and pulled her into the cupboard, closing the door quickly behind her.

Crinklebottom was clearly aggravated and sounding very concerned. He was walking with the Deputy Head Teachers.

'I don't care who it was, something isn't sitting right. I am not going to compromise this; the press conference will go ahead. No little blighter is going to spoil it for me.'

'They're just kids, they don't have the power to do anything, Sir.'

'Strange though' he spat back at her. 'Isn't it? Don't you think so? Six pupils join the school, midterm, at exactly the same time? I knew there was something fishy about it. I should have trusted my instincts. I want to know EVERYTHING there possibly is to know about the six of them. Try and get them to slip up and the moment they do, I want them in my office with their bags packed.'

Billy, Poppy and Gracie were barely breathing. They had their noses pressed up to the ridges in the door. Crinklebottom's hand fell onto one of the ridges, right in front of Billy's eyes. Billy dared not breathe or move a muscle. Crinklebottom pinched the ridge as if to open the door and then dusted his hand onto his black cape.

'And while you're at it, please will somebody ask Watson to dust the doorways in the corridor. The level of dust I've just pulled off those ridges is absolutely disgusting. I want to be able to lick the doorways.'

Billy, Gracie and Poppy looked around at each other, smiling. Poppy had to bite her knuckles to stop herself from laughing.

Crinklebum, Cabbagefeatures and Tuftybrowface all slinked up the corridor and out of earshot from the three of them stood in the cupboard.

'Looks like they are suspicious of us all,' Gracie said.

'Thought they would be,' Billy replied.

TWENTY-SIX

The five of them figured that since they all started at the school on the same day, it wouldn't seem suspicious that they would gravitate towards each other and spend time together on their first few days at the school.

They took their pencil cases and some posh art paper that they had found in the dormitory and took it down to a bench. They spoke mostly in whispers and pretended they were drawing pictures of the field and trees ahead of them.

'I'm not being funny Max,' Freddie said, 'that's the worst drawing I've ever seen.'

Max laughed and looked up at him. 'Yes, I never was very good at art,' he said, 'I'm right-handed you see.'

Freddie looked across at him awkwardly. Gracie wondered who would be the first to say it. Eventually she plucked up the courage...

'But you don't have a right hand, Max.'

Max laughed out loud. 'Exactly,' he said. 'That's why I'm so rubbish at drawing.'

'What happened?' Poppy asked, 'I mean, did you have an accident when you were little?'

Max was busy shading his picture with the various options

you can get out of a pencil, turning it to the side and pressing gently on the paper.

'No, I just wasn't born with it. At my Mum's first scan, they thought the umbilical cord might have got wrapped around my arm, but it turns out I've got this syndrome.'

'What's it called?' Billy asked.

'WAGR,' Max replied.

'Well, there's no need to be rude,' Billy said.

The five of them fell about laughing until the eldest, Gracie, reminded them to hush.

'It's okay,' Billy added, 'I can't hear that well remember.'

He put his hand up to his head, indicating his hearing aid. Isn't it odd, Gracie thought to herself? There they all were, all born with differences – here on the same mission.

'I was just thinking the same thing,' Billy said.

'I forgot you could do that,' Gracie smiled.

'I know my Mum and Dad were worried about whether people would accept me at school, or whether I'd be bullied for having a hearing aid.'

'Pardon?' Poppy said, overly loud. The five laughed again.

'Truth is, apart from the odd comment here and there, it just hasn't happened.'

'My Mum and Dad were the same,' Poppy said. 'You should see the pictures of me from when I was a baby.'

'You can barely see the scar on your lip,' Max said.

'I know, it's what makes me – me, though, I wouldn't change it.'

'So,' Gracie said, getting back to business 'let's go over what we have.'

The five agreed that 'CharlesDickensTale247,' 'FoxgloveNorth242left' and 'Wallshaveears247' combined with 'library,' 'walled-garden' and 'clocktower' were not the greatest clues in the world. In truth, it was hardly anything to go on.

'We've got time,' Freddie said.

'Are you joking?' Max replied. 'We've got until Tuesday at the latest. And we all know they're onto us.'

'We all need time to think,' Gracie said.

The five of them, for the first time in a long time, did no talking whatsoever. They just sat, thinking, using drawing as a welcome distraction from all of the world having fallen on their shoulders.

TWENTY-SEVEN

It seemed odd that none of the other pupils had made any effort with the five new people. There had been a couple of nods in the corridor from the prefects. It was almost as if everybody regarded them as 'misfits' who did not belong.

Or maybe human instinct had told everybody to stay away? Maybe all young people have superhuman powers with regards to things like that.

Perhaps they were all in on the efforts to shut down the school, but the five superheroes all agreed that this was highly improbable. The risk was that if one student had let it slip to their parents during a school holiday or a Sunday afternoon Facetime, Crinklebottom could have his bottom well and truly crinkled.

One thing the five of them did not have to moan about, was the food. Friday night supper was a delicious spread of burger buns, all the burger trimmings and burgers that looked like beef but were not, but to be fair, tasted delicious.

Billy had never understood that. If people chose to be vegetarian or vegan, he admitted that this was their choice and he supported it wholeheartedly. 'But why,' Billy said to his Mum one day over lunch, 'do they spend their whole lives trying to make things that don't look like meat - look like meat?'

His Mum was stumped. She mumbled something like 'Don't be rude Billy' with a mouth full of radishes and then stared out of a window, as parents do when they know their child is right but they do not know how to respond.

Max had his burger clasped in his hand. He held it up like a trophy, captain of the food team that had just won the world's first burger preparation competition. He looked at the burger like he had fallen in love and was just about to ask it to marry him.

'I've been waiting all day for you, you beautiful, beautiful thing. Get in my mouth NOW.'

Max brought the burger to his lips and as he did so, he realised that the dinner hall had fallen completely silent and everyone, including the teachers and the other superheroes, was sitting with their hands together and eyes closed - ready to pray.

The four others let out a snigger and Max dropped the burger onto his plate and fell into a prayer position instantaneously.

'When you've quite finished!' Crinklebottom barked across the room.

A brief silence and Max's cheeks flushed an embarrassed crimson colour.

'For what we are about to receive,' Crinklebottom declared, in true head teacher voice fashion, 'may the Universe make us truly thankful.'

'Amen' chanted the entire dinner hall. The five superheroes picked up their burgers and put them up to their mouths. Max had taken the most ginormous bite out of his.

'Okram Mitchum Declaronus!' Crinklebottom cried out

in monotones like a vicar who is close to retirement.

'Okram Mitchum Declaronus!' chanted the entire food hall back.

Max tried to chant with them but managed to spray Billy's entire front with bits of lettuce, tomato, guacamole and cheese as well as a few morsels of beef-but-not-beef over his tie.

'Magnamo elitis scandleaborough!' Crinklebottom shouted.

The hall repeated this second phrase. The most bizarre thing, it was not Latin - although it sounded vaguely similar.

Gracie turned to Poppy.

'What language are they speaking?' she whispered.

'I honestly don't understand it at all, haven't got a clue,' Poppy replied.

'Reeeetar Orrrramus Nott Siiiingatall!' Crinklebottom bellowed.

'Well,' Poppy said, 'if that was English, I think he just chanted "Rita Ora must not sing at all."'

'Seems a bit unfair,' Billy said, 'what's she done to upset him?'

Eventually, the chanting subsided, and they were able to eat without the fear of another phrase they had to guess and try and repeat back.

Again, Mrs Berry, still looking like a berry - but clearly towel dried from her Friday afternoon, staff room jacuzzi frenzy, walked around and collected the straw-like plates from the table. Likewise, Mr Walter was breaking them up into pieces and placing them in the trough outside.

'I've concluded that CharlesDickensTale142 and library have to go together,' Gracie said in a sort of whispered tone.

The other four agreed.

'There can't be that many Charles Dickens books in the

library. The first thing we should do at lights out is go and take a look.'

The other four disagreed, for a combination of reasons, from sheer terror to feeling a bit tired.

'Look,' Gracie added, 'out of the millions of kids in the country, we're here to do a job. I really don't want to have to go back to the Prime Minister's office having not done my best to solve the puzzle. Freddie is obviously key to all of this.'

'Oh, terrific.' Freddie said, sipping his plastic cup of cocoa. 'That's just great. Someone can have my device thingy this time, after all the trouble this afternoon.'

'It's lights out at 9:30pm,' Gracie said. 'I say the five of us meet outside where we were drawing earlier at 10:30pm?'

'I've got to get more used to these late nights and early starts.' Poppy said with a loud yawn.

'That's settled then,' Gracie said. 'See you then. Don't get caught.'

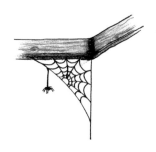

TWENTY-EIGHT

It took Billy's eyes about three or four minutes to adjust to the darkness, when the prefect had turned the lights out at 9:36pm. His bed was high enough for him to be able to see out of the window.

As his eyes were adjusting, he saw a spider scuttle across the ceiling and begin building a web in the corner of the room. It danced from side to side, spinning more and more threads.

Billy had never considered being jealous of a spider before. All of a sudden, the prospect of building a quick bed and then settling down for the night seemed quite appealing. Maybe he just wasn't cut out for all of this. Of all the kids in his class at school, he was the last person he would choose for such a mission. He was pleased, proud even, to be part of it - but the eels slithering around in his stomach with nervousness would beg to differ.

Worst of all, he hated avocados and the brave decision at dinner to add guacamole to his beef-lookalike burger meant that every time he burped, he felt like his throat was growing an avocado tree.

With all of the spider watching and dinner regurgitating he had lost track of time completely. He looked over at his bedside table. It was 10:10 on the digital clock, he thought he'd watch it until 10:11 and then rest his eyes for a few moments.

A second after 10:11, the clock went blank. Billy sat, bolt upright. The lamps outside the window had been plunged into darkness, so too had the light trickling through the door frame from the corridor.

Excellent, he thought, the power's out. That'll be helpful.

What felt like around ten minutes later, he slowly sat up and moved to the side of the bed, trying to avoid the creaks and pops as he moved. The old cliché of the person in the bed next door snoring and turning loudly caused him to panic and he stopped still.

He placed one foot and then the other into his slippers and fastened his dressing gown.

'The route was simple enough,' he'd been thinking to himself all evening. Straight out of the dormitory door and down the grand stone staircase, meet the others at the bottom.

Something about it felt uneasy, though. Who knew if there might be teachers or prefects on duty in and around the staircase? He didn't have enough experience to second guess, if he or the others were caught - it was game over.

He looked out of the old sash window at the roof beneath. It was a four foot drop at the most to the roof of the kitchens below. The building looked old and sturdy enough to withstand his weight and after all, he was used to jumping out of windows these days.

The noise of the creaky dormitory door would far outweigh the window being raised up, surely? He raised his arm up and parted the golden latch from the top of the window. Then he placed his finger under the metal loop at the bottom and raised it slowly.

Almost silent. Apart from the noise in the wooden frame, there were no squeaks or pops at all. Glancing up, Billy saw that even the spider was still happy to dance away and weave without being disturbed.

He sat up on the window ledge and moved his legs from in the room to outside in one swift movement. He was becoming an 'escape from bedroom' professional these days and this time, there was far less open space to jump down.

'What are you doing?' came a half-asleep voice from across the room.

Billy's bum left the window and shot about a foot in the air, causing him to bump his head on the top of the lifted frame.

'Sorry. I was just feeling a bit warm,' Billy replied.

'Close the window. It's freezing in here.' came the tired voice.

Billy turned around to face the enemy and saw the boy in stripy green pyjamas, with an eye mask over his eyes, half-sitting-half-lying with his head facing in Billy's direction.

'Alright. I'm sorry,' Billy said.

'Such an idiot,' came the reply from Stripy, who turned his body and curled up onto the other side of his bed, pulling the duvet up to his neck, his eye mask unmoved.

Billy leaned back into the room, to make sure his voice came from inside and not out.

'Night then,' Billy muttered in a whisper.

'Shut up and go to sleep!' ranted the stripy-green, eye-masked boy.

And with that, Billy slid out of the window and closed it sharply behind him. He did not peer back through to check that Stripy's eye mask was still securely fastened around his head, it would be too late anyway.

He crawled along the roof, underneath several other dormitory windows and then reached a sheer drop, as the roof ended.

Now what? He thought to himself. Jumping down, was definitely not a considered option in the same way as it had been at home that night. Thankfully, an old Victorian gutter came to the rescue this time. It almost looked like it had been built as an escape route, with strong metal rods pinning it to the wall.

Billy could climb down it easily and began doing so, until three steps down he heard that old distinctive voice of Crinklebum again. Billy kept deadly still.

Crinklebottom was whistling and dancing along the pathway, eating what looked to Billy like a slice of toast. Without warning, he broke out into song.

'One four severrrrn, one four severrrrn, you genius...yes you are, yes you are.'

He scuttled from one side of the pathway to the other, like he was rehearsing an appearance on Dancing on Ice. If he saw Billy now, it would be the end of everything. Luckily, he was so wrapped up in himself with everything he did - there was no way he was going to look up at any point.

Billy finished his great escape and cautiously moved around the pathway until he could see his superhero counterparts, stood underneath the stairwell, awaiting his arrival.

He tapped gently on the window and Max opened the fire exit with his left arm and let him in.

'Nice of you to join us' said Gracie.

The corridors seemed dangerously safe. They were quiet and desolate and there was no light because of the power cut. But the silence was eerie. It was like a horror film when you know somebody could jump out at any second. But nobody did.

It felt weird that the five of them walked, almost in a straight line, slap bang through the centre.

Poppy thought to herself, in all the films, we'd be scuttling around the edge and hiding behind things. Billy whispered to her, 'It's funny that, Gracie was thinking the same thing just a moment ago.' Poppy looked at him and smiled at him, thinking, imagine a naked grandma...

'Eurgh,' said Billy, 'stop it.'

'That'll teach you.' she spat back at him.

'Where's Watson's office?' said Freddie.

'Just down here,' Gracie said, pointing, 'I went to find it earlier after dinner.'

'I can go in and get the library key, but I'm going to need you to do something to distract him. Nobody wants to see a key rising up by itself from the key box and disappearing out of a doorway. He'll have a heart attack.'

Watson's office was right next to a large cupboard marked, 'Danger of death, keep out'

'We'll wait here.' said Gracie.

Freddie disappeared into the cupboard and there was a brief silence.

Billy leaned ever so slightly left so that he could peer inside the office. Gracie pulled him back sharply. In a millisecond, Billy saw Watson sitting with his feet up on the desk away from the door. A half eaten chocolate bar was in his hand and the caramel at the end of it was dripping into a large pile of dust onto the floor. The walls were covered in a vast array of blue plastic boxes piled high with screws, nuts and bolts.

'I think he might be asleep,' Billy said.

'We can't risk it,' Max replied, leaning over his shoulder.

With that, Max scuttled across the corridor to the other side where there was a large scaffold tower. He looked back over at the three others and pointed at the 'danger of death' cupboard, indicating the others should go inside. The three did so instantly, closing the door behind them as gently as they could.

Through the gaps in the door they could see Max lifting the entire scaffold tower in the air with his one arm, at least six inches off the floor and dropping it back down again, then running as fast as he could down the corridor and out of view. Mr Watson appeared with his torch just several seconds afterwards. He hesitantly moved towards the scaffold tower, inspecting the various bolts and screws up and down the tower.

Whilst he did so, a small, singular, silver key moved through the air out of Watson's office and swiftly down the corridor. Gracie pumped her fist in the air. Billy dodged out of the way of it and then looked up at the very large electrical switchboard on the wall. Everything was labelled with small strips of masking tape.

Billy noticed that the 'main lights' big red lever was switched towards 'off.' He tapped Gracie and Poppy on the shoulder and pointed at it.

'Someone's done that on purpose,' he whispered.

Wats-his-face-on had disappeared back into his office now, the three of them gave it a few seconds before quietly exiting and following the trail of the dancing key in the corridor.

When they reached the doorway at the end, Freddie was standing there having fully morphed back into a visible human.

'That's four,' Poppy said with a smile.

Just then Max appeared on the other side of the door, looking red faced and out of breath.

'That's five,' Gracie said, 'come on let's do this.'

TWENTY-NINE

The large library was in a building all of its own. The hall itself was probably six times the size of Billy's house. The key that Freddie had retrieved seemed a bit pathetic all of a sudden. He handed it to Gracie who put it in the lock and opened the door.

The five superheroes stepped inside and glared at the walls covered in books from floor to ceiling.

'Right,' Max said, 'where's Dickens?'

They didn't have to wander far to find the authors with a surname beginning with 'D.'

'Didn't he write the one about that orphan?' Poppy asked.

'Oliver Twist,' answered Gracie.

'What other books?' Max said running his hand along the shelf, 'Great Expectations, A Tale of Two Cities...'

'Stop!' shouted Billy. 'CharlesDickensTale142. Open the book.'

Max blew a sheet of dust and it flew through the air and made Gracie sneeze.

'Cut it out Max, seriously,' she said before sneezing a second time.

He opened the book. Nothing. They waited for something

to happen. Nothing did, except a dead fly fell down from inside the cover and fell onto Max's shoe.

'Well, not that one then,' Max said.

'Try page 147,' Billy said, remembering Crinklebum's little ditty as he danced down the pathway just minutes earlier.

Max leafed through and found page 147. There was a long pause. Billy could hear everybody else breathing. His heart sank and he was bitterly disappointed. He thought he'd solved the riddle. What on earth was it going to be now?

Max unpicked the ribbon bookmark attached to the book and placed it down the middle of page 147, before closing the book and returning it to the shelf, in a different place from where it was previously.

'Not there, two on from that,' Gracie said crossly.

'As if they'll notice that,' Max said, sniggering.

He moved the book along two places and put it back in the shelf. There was a large creaking sound.

'Someone's coming!' Poppy screamed.

'That's coming from in there.' Gracie said.

'In where?' asked Billy.

The bookcase shook ever so slightly and before every book fell off the shelf, the bookcase moved backwards by itself and slotted into the wall behind, revealing a gloomy, narrow stairwell.

Max's sunken heart had come back to life and had almost leapt out of his chest, ran around the top of his head a bit and leapt back in. He distinctly felt the avocado tree in his throat sprout back out and he thought he was going to throw up.

Without saying a word to one another, the five began the slow descent into nothingness. Max was leading the way, with Poppy following closely. Gracie went next, with Freddie's hand on her shoulder. Billy did not want to be last down, but he found himself wandering slightly behind the others. It was not that he wanted to be first, or cared about being last, he just knew that being at the back means you are the first to get caught if there is someone behind you.

The brickwork was damp, as if there was a leaky pipe somewhere and the spiral staircase seemed to go on forever. At the bottom of the steps, there was barely enough room for one person, let alone the five of them.

Rather than a host of secret passageways, a large room or a secret hideaway, all that lay at the bottom of the stairwell was a solitary book with a red leather cover.

Max read it out, as he was the only one who could fit in the tiny space to retrieve it. 'A Tale of Two Cities' he read slowly. 'It's the same thing.'

As he slowly opened it, there were not hundreds of pages of the great Charles Dickens' words. Within it were just a host of empty pages. Max flicked through them all as quickly as he could. When he got about two thirds of the way through, there was a list written in thick black ink.

It was not English. Billy recognised one of the languages as possibly French, but he could not be sure.

Max handed the book to Poppy.

'This one's for you,' he said pushing it into Poppy's hands.

Poppy studied it. There are at least eleven languages in here, she thought to herself.

As Billy was the only one who could hear this thought he asked her, 'And will you be able to work out what it is?'

'I'll need some time, some of the language is hard to make out. I'm pretty sure this bottom one is Arabic, but the handwriting is so awful, I can't really tell.'

'We'd better take it with us then,' Freddie said.

'You must be joking,' Gracie replied. 'We take that, they'll search the building from top to bottom tomorrow. We can't risk that.'

'We'll give you some time,' Billy said, 'how long do you need?'

'An hour or so, I think,' Poppy replied, studying the words on the page and moving the book backwards and forwards with her eyes.

'We'll wait up there,' Gracie said.

'Alright, throw me down a pen!'

Poppy squeezed past Max and slid her back down the wall so she was sat down. The others wandered back up the spiral stairs and waited.

THIRTY

Considering how boring it is sitting and doing absolutely nothing, an hour seemed to pass incredibly quickly.

Max delighted them all with his choice of one liner jokes and everybody huffed and puffed at how awful they were. The only joke that had them in stitches was when he said, 'What's E.T. short for?'

'We don't know Max,' said an exasperated Gracie, 'what is E.T. short for?'

'Because he's got little legs!' said Max giggling, before he finished the punch line.

It took a while for the joke to sink in but after a few moments, the four of them were in hysterics.

Poppy appeared at the top of the staircase, with beads of sweat dripping from her forehead.

'Are you alright?' Billy asked.

'Yeah,' Poppy replied, 'it got hot down there after a while.'

'And?' Gracie asked.

'Yes, I've done it. It's a list of ingredients for the packaging. I don't really know what any of them are, it's all phosphates and sulphates mostly, but I've got it.'

'Excellent,' Gracie said, adding, 'let's phone the PM.'

They managed to put everything back to normal. Max, Poppy and Gracie went up to their respective dormitories and Billy had the unfortunate task of accompanying Freddie to return the library key.

As he waited in the cupboard for him, he heard a mobile phone ring. He recognised that it was the first mobile phone bleep he had heard since he had been inside Finian's. He panicked at first that it was Freddie's device again, then he heard the voice of Mr Watson.

'I've got the answer for you, yes.' Billy heard. He pinned his good ear as close to the wall as he could.

'The answer is, completely obliterated. The whole thing. Twenty years it's taken me. Twenty years and now...'

Billy heard Watson's voice crack like he was about to cry.

'I'm sorry I'm getting upset. I'm just not paid enough for them to take away my...I know, I know...but it means a lot to me....yeah, see you tomorrow.'

And with that he hung up the phone. When he turned around Freddie was stood in the doorway and Billy jumped out of his skin again.

'You scared the living daylights out of me.'

Freddie placed his finger over his mouth and gave Billy a look reminding him to shut up.

'I have to see what he's thinking,' Billy said.

'Why?'

'I just need to know what that phone call was about.'

Billy and Freddie stepped out of the electrical cupboard and Billy crept towards the doorway. He could see Watson running his finger along the office worktop and staring out of the window into the darkness.

Billy broke his gaze and walked briskly back up the corridor. Freddie rushed to join him.

'Well,' Freddie whispered, 'what was he thinking?'

'He was thinking of foxgloves,' Billy replied.

'What are they?' Freddie asked.

But Billy did not reply. He kept moving forward, deep in thought.

THIRTY-ONE

However weird and odd this whole experience was, opening your tired eyes on a Saturday morning and facing the prospect of putting your school uniform on, was something so annoying that Billy could barely contain his anger.

He was so filled with rage, he put his uniform on in a rigid routine, as if he were in the army. His arms were straight, his torso was straight, when brushing his hair - he stood straight.

When he brushed his teeth, he stood straight. When he spat the contents of the toothpaste and spit out of his mouth, he stood straight. When he had to dab the spit and toothpaste off his blazer because he had missed the bowl completely, making him even more annoyed - he still stood straight.

Nobody else seemed in the slightest bit bothered. Everyone else in the dormitory, including Freddie, was alert and happy and just getting on with things as if nothing were wrong at all.

Saturdays were for the following:

Telling your Mum and Dad that you definitely didn't have homework set for the weekend.

Sitting on the sofa in just your dressing gown (or just your pants in summer months), watching pointless TV.

Sighing, huffing and puffing continuously when Mum or

Dad (usually Mum) tells you that you HAVE to get dressed.

He imagined his Mum and Dad sat outside at the wooden table, sipping their morning coffee. Dad would be reading the paper and moaning about this, that and the other and Mum would be telling him repeatedly to, 'calm down and get a life.'

As he stared into the mirror, he felt a lump appear in his throat. He tried to swallow it back down and as he did so, his eyes filled with tears. This was not a physical lump at all, it was a 'miss you Mum and Dad' lump. As he stared at himself in the mirror, he wondered if that disappears when you get older - or if you always miss them when you're away?

Max knew what he was getting at, he too looked annoyed on the way to the assembly hall. His tie was misshapen and his trousers were not properly over his shoes, it was clear he had not wanted to get out of bed either.

The Saturday morning assembly was as dull as any assembly ever is, times a million.

The stupid school chants went on and on forever, there was no explanation as to what they were chanting about — or why.

It was only when Crinklebuttocks introduced the first hymn and announced he was going to put some pictures on a PowerPoint presentation, to remind the pupils how important nature was, that the lightbulb went off in Billy's head.

'All of the aforementioned photographs,' declared Crinkle, 'have actually been taken here in the grounds, by our very own Mr Watson.'

Whilst mumbling through the words of the hymn, Billy could see the various pictures flashing up. It was only because Crinkly had been so pedantic about the labelling of each photograph that Billy had his lightbulb moment.

A picture of the meadow flashed up on the screen and the

label underneath read 'Foxglove' and then an explanation of the plant followed underneath, including the caption, 'highly dangerous for animals and humans.'

Billy looked up at Crinklebottom who was singing from his hymn book. His singing voice was loud and proud, but he could not quite place each note, making him sound very out of tune with the organ. In fact, thought Billy, he sounded like an angry lion with an upset stomach.

As the foxglove flashed up his eyes met with Crinkle's. He heard every word he was thinking, Yes, highly toxic, so you can ALL keep well away. Then his thoughts did a sort of evil laugh, like you hear the evil king do in fairy tale books as a young child.

It was so odd, that Billy could not help but wince. The startled Crinklebottom shot an incredibly fierce look at Billy and stopped mentally laughing immediately.

THIRTY-TWO

Kind, courteous and lovely were not three words that Billy had associated with this experience so far.

But Mrs Browning happened to be all of these things. She should have retired about thirty years ago, she was so old. None of them had ever seen her before.

It was weird and slightly odd, that the five superheroes had been put in the same class on a Saturday morning.

'Is it a bit weird that it's just us?' Gracie asked Poppy.

'You mean, they're trying to keep us out of the way?' Poppy said back.

Before Gracie answered, Mrs Browning had entered the room. She was holding the largest mug you have ever seen and sipped from it several times.

'That's a lot of coffee,' Max commented.

'That liquid's clear, it's not coffee.' Gracie whispered to him.

'How can you...? Oh yes, seeing through things, I forgot you could do that...a big cup of water then.'

Mrs Browning let out a ginormous burp and seemed to trip over her shoelace into her seat in the middle of the room.

'Or maybe gin,' Max added.

Gracie sniggered, which was sharply interrupted by Mrs B. 'Hello my dears, I know I'm old, tired and so is my voice. I'm Mrs Browning and I've worked at this school my entire life. Sixty years to be exact. They still pay me to come in on Saturdays and teach you all general studies. So, what would you like to learn about today?'

'You mean it's up to us, Miss?' asked Freddie.

'General studies is what it says on the tin, young man. It could mean anything or everything. Many of the hundreds of pupils who have sat before you call my classes the University of Life. Be careful though, some also called it a pointless waste of time. Let's do the class, then you can decide what to believe.'

The next thirty minutes felt like thirty seconds as Mrs Browning told countless stories of her life as a teacher. All five of them really liked her and were disappointed when the lesson came to an end.

'So, remember dears,' she concluded, 'friends are like stars. You may not always be able to see them, but you always know they are there.'

The class ended and the five of them found themselves outside wondering what had just happened.

'Right, let's get out of these stupid uniforms and then I need to speak to you all about FoxgloveNorth242Left,' Billy said.

Half an hour later, the five of them were sat in more comfortable clothes and Billy was explaining his theory about the foxglove meadow.

'The thing is, the more I've thought about it, the more it makes sense,' he said.

'Whereabouts is this field?' asked Max.

'Over by the main entrance,' Gracie interrupted.

'There's something there,' Billy added, 'I'm certain of it,

the question is...where?'

'North 242 left,' pondered Poppy.

'It could mean anything,' Max said. 'The field's big, I'll give you that, but 242 steps in any direction would take you out of the foxglove meadow and into somewhere else beyond.'

'The thing is, the site is covered with wildlife.' Gracie said.

'Exactly,' Billy interjected. 'And that's the thing, hiding anything in that field would be certain to keep animals and humans away.'

'What makes it so toxic?' Max asked.

'It has stuff in it that slows your heart rate down,' Billy replied. 'I googled it. So whatever we do, we need to avoid getting any of it in our mouths.'

'I wasn't planning on eating it,' Gracie said.

'Whatever we do, we can't do it now, we'll definitely get caught.' Billy said.

'It'll have to be tomorrow morning?' Poppy suggested. '5am?'

Max was the last to agree to it and took a little persuading, but they got there eventually.

THIRTY-THREE

At 4am on Sunday morning, Billy was wide awake. He was getting used to the late nights and early mornings now. The graceful spider had woven a mansion on the ceiling since the previous night. He had also brought his wife and kids with him and was enjoying a tasty fly that he had caught in the top room of his humble abode. The fly had been spun by bits of web and was dangling by several threads off the side.

Billy's mind had been so busy that he had not really contemplated what would happen if the five of them got caught. The fear of seeing the tangled spider was all too much and he started to imagine what Crinklebum would do if his plans for global media stardom were thwarted and the government would not be able to get to them in time to save them.

Corporal punishment had been banned many years earlier, so surely, they would not be physically beaten. But what about if they were mentally tortured, or worse still, had to face the sentence of staying at Finian's any longer than was physically necessary. The five of them might have some degree of superpower, but that did not stop you feeling physical and emotional pain.

Billy realised, for the first time, that life would never be the same after all this. Stopping and thinking about it for more than five seconds became totally overwhelming and he felt that same lump in his throat again that he had felt in the morning when thinking of his Mum and Dad.

Billy slipped on some comfortable clothes, he actually could not tell if they would be comfortable at all – he had never worn them before. But they had looked it several days before, in the Prime Minister's office.

The trendy plimsolls, the sort your Mum always refuses to buy you when you are out shopping, rubbed a little on his heel but the pain wore off after a while.

'Who's up?' the rumbling tones of Eye Patch came from the bed across the dormitory.

'It's Billy, I don't feel well, I'm heading down to the member of staff on duty.'

'You. Again. Well, keep the noise down...and don't throw up on the floor, it's impossible to mop up and I'm on cleaning duty today.'

'Right you are,' replied Billy, thinking to himself, thanks for the sympathy, you eye-patch-wearing monster.

That was a gamble. Billy did not expect for one second that Eye-Patch would even remember the conversation when he woke up, but if he did and he happened to talk to a teacher, that could give the game away.

Ah well, Billy thought to himself, I don't have any choice.

Light was pouring in through the stained glass windows in the main stairwell. If this were a hotel and Billy had been staying in it with his family, it would have given him that lovely Sunday morning feeling where anything seems possible. But at this moment in time, very little seemed possible. Those eels were back in his stomach again, churning and begging to be fed by more gulps of fear.

Instead, Billy gave his stomach a few little punches, which at least moved the eels around a little for a few seconds.

Once he had moved into the second corridor, he could see the glow of light coming from Watsit's office. Outside the door were about twenty metal cans, about the size of a box of crisps. They were stacked perfectly, with a white label across the front of each 'BF,' scrawled in marker pen.

'Ah, there's the biofuel,' Billy thought to himself.

Carefully walking past the door, he saw Watson in the same position as the previous time, feet up on the worktop and slumped in his chair snoring away like a steam train. Billy wondered to himself what it would be like to sleep in a plastic chair every single night. Pretty uncomfortable, was his conclusion.

There was one final door to navigate before Billy was out in the open air. He lifted the latch, praying to the deity of doors that he would not need WD40 to stop the squeaks and pops of the wood.

It opened seamlessly, with a slight creak – but the echo seemed to bellow outwards into the open air.

There was a soft whirring sound in the distance, which sounded like it was growing closer by the millisecond. Imagine if a bumblebee grew an engine? That is what the sound was like, the cross between a buzz and the sort of motorbike that delivers pizza.

This unnerved Billy and he hid behind one of the many plant pots that were covering the patio area immediately outside the door. Crouching down, a vehicle came around the corner incredibly quickly. Was it hovering or travelling along the gravel? It certainly was not churning the stones the way a car tyre would. Although it probably was not that quick, it seemed to pass Billy and the plant pot at a hundred miles an hour. There was somebody in control of the vehicle. It certainly was not Crinklebottom, the person was not nearly tall enough – even in a sitting position he could see that. So, who was it?

'I'd better warn the others,' Billy said out loud quietly, thinking to himself, this is turning into a Hollywood film, I'm actually talking to myself out loud. Weirdo.

As he reached the base of the meadow, the others had already arrived as usual.

The five of them made two hundred and forty-two steps forwards. It took longer than expected, they went way beyond the foxglove plantation and were into a nearby field. At exactly the number of steps specified, there was nothing but a small patch of grass and a nearby stream. The five of them searched high and low for some sort of clue or piece of the puzzle that they had not seen, but there was nothing.

'Right, it's back to the start then,' Gracie said.

'Happy Sunday morning to you too,' groaned Max, rubbing his eyes.

At the start point, just about to set off, Billy stopped.

'Wait,' he commanded. The other four stopped, startled. They had never heard Billy talk with that assertiveness before.

'Let's try twenty-four steps forward and then two steps to the left,' he added.

It was a mixture between spring and summer and five o'clock in the morning and was still relatively chilly. In all honesty, the five of them were willing to try anything to get out of the cold.

After completing the steps, Freddie pointed at a patch of grass that was slightly more overgrown amidst all of the foxglove shrubbery.

'There's a metal cover underneath,' Gracie said, 'I can see it through the grass.'

Freddie and Poppy rushed over and tried to prize the large piece of metal up from the ground.

'There's no way we're moving that,' Poppy said, struggling to breathe.

Billy turned to Max, who smiled and walked over to the cover. He pulled at the metal, it lifted a fraction off the floor and fell back down again. He reached into his pocket and grabbed a small capsule of EMC249 and bit the cap off the top of it, spitting it onto the floor. He downed the few mouthfuls of liquid, waited about ten seconds, let out a giant burp and then wiped his mouth with his sleeve. He leant forwards and grabbed the piece of metal with his only arm and lifted it a foot from the floor and placed it down in a patch of grass.

The slab of metal was so heavy that it instantly flattened the grass, so there was no distinction between the ground and the metal. The weight of it sank straight into the meadow floor.

Much like they had the previous day in the library, the five of them stared into the black darkness, just a few steps visible near the top.

As they slowly ventured down, the space grew darker and darker. Why nobody thought to bring a torch was beyond any of them. A mobile phone would have done it, but since none of them had brought one down (what's the point, you can't get signal anywhere, anyway) they were left with nothing.

The five of them could make out a small amount of light ahead of them which indicated that there was a corner coming up.

'Corner ahead,' Gracie said.

There was not enough space for them to walk in a line of

five, but they could just about fit two-by-two. There was some comfort in this. Gracie and Max were at the front, walking cautiously. Poppy and Billy walked just behind, Poppy with her hand on Gracie's shoulder. Freddie was at the back, just a few steps behind the others.

As they turned the corner, Gracie and Max fell backwards and like a set of dominoes almost fell to the floor, almost taking Poppy and Billy down with them.

Light was coming from a lantern, which was being held up...by Mrs Browning.

THIRTY-FOUR

That was it then, their entire mission scrambled. They were at the cusp of absolute greatness and here they were, discovered in the middle of it all, by the drunk old woman who had burped her neat gin throughout an hour of general studies the previous morning.

She looked like an old oil painting. There were so many wrinkles in her face, it was as if every night, someone came and gave her face a scrunch up - the same way you would if you took your anger out on a piece of A4 paper but flattened it out again afterwards.

'Well, well, well. Now, I ask you my dears…what would the five new pupils who are new to the school, be doing in here, so early in the morning?' she spoke softly, menacingly, like the danger in her voice was going to keep growing.

'We could ask you the same question, Mrs Browning.' Max said boldly and bravely. If the game was up, he thought to himself, we're going to go out with a bang.

'Please,' she replied. 'It's Elsie Browning now. It's five in the morning, I'm not a teacher. Today my boy, I'm a security guard.'

'What are you guarding?' Poppy asked.

'Don't insult my intelligence, young lady. You know jolly well what I'm guarding, and I know jolly well that you're down here trying to find it.'

'Well if you knew we were coming' Billy said, 'why didn't you try and stop us earlier?'

'You're down here,' Browning snapped back, 'for the biofuel recipe.'

'Yes, this school is trying to thwart the British government,' Billy yelled.

'Excellent use of the word thwart,' Mrs B replied.

'Thanks Miss.' Billy embarrassingly looked down at his plimsolls, covered in mud and shards of foxglove, pulling the same face he did when he put his hand up and answered one of Mrs Clinch's questions.

'So, what's your plan?' she said, looking up from her lantern and thrusting it in the direction of all five pupils, growing more nervous by the second.

'We're obviously not going to tell you that,' Gracie muttered, adding 'you'll just tell Crinklefeatures.'

'Mr CrinkleBOTTOM is the finest headmaster this school has ever seen young lady,' she snapped at him. Then she brought the lantern up to her face and the wrinkles seemed to change shape all of a sudden, the frown turned into an evil glare. 'Or at least, he was.'

The five superheroes, who had been holding their breath, all let out the air in their lungs at the same time, in one big exhalation.

'I've been working here for sixty years. One might even say, I'm part of the fabric of the building, the furniture – if you like. The school knows everything there is to know about me. They know I have two sons, one of whom lives overseas. They know I lost my husband twelve years back and they even gifted me a cottage on the far side of the school grounds for my many years of service. They know everything they possibly could, except one tiny fact.'

She leant forward for dramatic effect bringing the gas lamp so close to her face, it almost singed her facial hair.

'I have…a brother.'

Billy looked over at Max, who was probably pulling the same face that he was pulling. A face that says, who cares that you've got a brother? And why is that relevant, now?

'You see, when I started working here, my brother and I had a huge disagreement over boring family stuff. That meant, every time family came up as a topic of conversation, I chose not to mention him. As time passed and we reconnected with one another, it became an ongoing joke between him and I. How long could I hide him from view? The answer is, I always have. He even visited my little cottage on my 60th birthday and STILL nobody at the school knows who he is, or that we're related. After my own husband died, my brother and I became incredibly close and talk every day on the phone about…everything really.'

'I'm really sorry, but I just don't get how this is relevant?' Poppy said, just as confused as the other four.

'It is no accident that I'm on security duty down here tonight, young lady.'

A long silence followed. None of them knew what to say next, or how to get out of this without fearing for their lives. Max put his hand in his pocket to activate the button on his device, to at least start the process of being rescued.

'Hands out of your pockets please young man!' she shrieked at him. 'There's no need to activate that device now.'

Brilliant, Billy thought to himself. Not only do they know about their plans, they also know about the devices that they've been given, they probably knew about the library break-in, this was turning into a living nightmare. His stomach eels were ready to burst out and eat Browning's gas lamp for breakfast.

Mrs Browning looked at each and every one of the superheroes and suddenly smiled.

'The fact is, that for the first time on these premises, I am going to reveal my brother's identity to five people I barely know. My brother is the Prime Minister. The very best of luck to you all.'

With that, Mrs Browning placed her gas lamp down on the floor and scuttled past the five superheroes, patting Billy on the back as she awkwardly steered her body around them all.

'But then, why didn't he just ask you for all of this information?' Billy asked.

Mrs Browning turned around.

'He did, of course dear boy. But as I explained to him, it would've looked incredibly suspect if I suddenly began making an appearance at staff meetings and breaking into libraries and stealing recipes. I don't have the skills to see inside that envelope down there.'

She pointed at a small green bottle on the floor.

'Smashing that bottle would have led them back to me, instantly. The game would've been up before it began. Whereas, all five of you, have a real fighting chance. I wish you every success.'

With that, she scuttled off again, into the darkness.

Nobody opened their mouth, until she had completely gone.

THIRTY-FIVE

The five superheroes peered into the murky green bottle. Inside, was just a single slip of paper.

It had been rolled up to be put inside, but had unrolled itself partially in the bottle itself, so they could make out some scribbled words in the same leaky ink as the previous list.

Max grabbed the bottle and clenched it in his left hand. With a view to breaking the glass, he tightened his grip and took a deep breath in. His face contorted and as he held his breath, he put all his mental strength and energy into his left hand.

'Don't do that,' shouted Gracie, 'pass it here, I'll be able to see through it.

She examined the bottle for several minutes.

'Yes, I can read it. Like in the library, it's a list of ingredients. I don't understand what any of them are. Ethanol is here. Vegetable oil...erm, orange peel?'

Poppy took a small notebook from her back pocket and wrote down the list of ingredients. After she'd written the list down, she gave it to Gracie to check off.

Billy picked up Mrs Browning's gas lamp and led the walk back down the tunnel with the four others following closely behind. Max leapt ahead and pushed up the metal cover, moving it out of the way, so that the others could climb the stairs, to the fresh air above.

The sky was much lighter now, the sun had come up over the trees behind the foxglove meadow and the five felt quite vulnerable to others who may walk past, at any minute. It took a few seconds for their eyes to adjust.

'So, just the one left then,' Poppy said.

'Yes,' remarked Gracie, 'wallshaveears247. I have to say I'm totally stumped.'

'And we're running out of time,' Max interrupted.

'We've got the whole day,' Billy said.

There was a sense of relief that they had now found two of the three things they were looking for, so despite their anxiousness to get the job done, there was a sense of calmness in the group that there had not been before.

'This is just a list of ingredients, right?' Freddie said.

'Two lists of ingredients,' Gracie added.

'When you buy a chocolate bar, all of the ingredients are on the back right?' he replied.

'So?' Max said, sarcastically.

'Thing is, it's not about the ingredients is it?' Freddie said, like he was onto something. 'Famous chocolate companies tell you their ingredients, but they don't tell you how they bung them all together. It's like they give you the ingredients but you can't recreate the magic recipe unless you're one of the chosen few.'

'Alright, what's your point Freddie?' Gracie snapped at him.

'The third bit must be the way it's all put together, what is mixed with what, and when...' Freddie said, like he was revealing the winning lottery numbers.

'He's got a point,' Billy said in agreement. 'All of this stuff is useless if you don't know how much of it and where it all goes.'

'So, what do we do now?' asked Poppy.

'I know time is a big issue for us,' Gracie said, 'but I think we're going to have to waste a bit of it blending in with everybody el-'

Before she had finished her sentence, a huge air raid siren started sounding. The five of them noticed loudspeakers at several points at the side of the buildings. It was the sort of speakers you get at a school fete, you know the ones when people announce what time the dance demonstration is, or tell everyone to 'Make sure they try the hook-a-duck and tombola.'

'What on earth is that?' Max said, putting his hand over his left ear.

'Attention all students' came the booming, but slightly crackly voice of Crinklebottom from the speaker. Let's refer to him as cracklebum, for ease. The speaker bounced to the sound of his annoying voice, like it was a partygoer at an all-night rave.

'All students must immediately report to the assembly hall, WITHOUT fail,' Cracklebum said, half angrily - the other half defiantly. The bouncy speaker rested.

The five of them looked at each other. Had Mrs Browning been lying? Had she gone straight to Cracklebum and told him everything?

They stood, brushing the bits of foxglove, mud and dirt from their legs, elbows and bums and all five, tentatively headed for the assembly hall. On their journey, they noticed several security vans, with people up ladders fitting what looked like cameras onto the wall.

Cracklecrinklebum was stood in the doorway. Ignoring the fact it was Sunday, he was still dressed in his three piece suit, with his black cape draped over his shoulders. His tie seemed a little looser than normal. There was a tiny glint of panic in his eye and he gave the falsest smile to the superheroes as they approached the doorway.

'I'm glad to see that you five found one another,' he commented as they approached. 'How...nice, that the five of you have connected, being new.'

None of them said a word, they just moved past him as quickly as they possibly could and took their seats in the great hall.

There was a far more relaxed mood. Nobody wore school uniform and because of their complete innocence, hundreds of young people were sat chatting to one another. The loud hubbub of noise was a mixture of jokes and banter, that demonstrated loads of friends who were used to spending their only day off in the grounds of their school.

The sound was gradually reduced to silence, as Crinklecracklebum wandered through the aisle to the front of the hall.

THIRTY-SIX

'Silence!' Crinklebottom bellowed, raising his hand up as if he was going to break out into interpretative dance.

Billy thought this was completely pointless, there was already absolute silence in the room. Another example of a stupid power trip, he thought to himself, whilst he stared down at his toes.

He looked up and stared at Crinkle. Today will not end, without me discovering the culprit, focus Bartholomew, what you say now could be vital, Crinkle was thinking.

Billy sniggered audibly and tried to cover it up with a cough. He couldn't wait to tell his new found friends that Cracklecrinkle's first name was actually Bartholomew.

'Someone here should be called guilty!' he shouted. 'Someone here is feeling pretty proud of themself. Someone is sitting here now, proud of the fact that they've slipped out of their dormitory during the night and visited the library.'

The five were careful not to exchange glances, or look at one another. Like five, poker-faced detectives, they sat and stared, just like every other pupil was doing.

Personally, Billy was relieved that he only knew about the library.

'As you all know, the world for all of us, is at the peak of change - at all times. Nobody in this school is above the rules. For that reason, the security team we work with are placing additional cameras around the school grounds. Until this morning, we had just twenty-four cameras around the perimeter school site - and seven infrared cameras, protecting us all at nighttime. Until now, we felt no need to have cameras in the school itself. By the end of this afternoon, there will be an additional ten cameras placed in various positions for our safety and security.'

Another lightbulb dinged in Billy's head. 247. Twenty-four cameras and seven infrared, he thought to himself. Twenty-four-seven.

Crinklebottom lowered his tone, to a more evil and sinister sound. 'Of course, if the culprit wanted to come forward to me privately, I would like to publicly say that the punishment will be reduced to litter duty for one week. After all, reading is not a crime and I applaud anybody for visiting the library. However, it is strictly out of bounds and against the school policy to visit it out of hours. If the culprit doesn't come forward and I find out who it is, they will be expelled.'

There were a few murmurs and mini gasps from the pupils. However stern Crinklebottom was, expelling people had not been his style. He chose his victims carefully and if he didn't like them, he would make their lives hell at school and bully them throughout their time. 'Better to keep and bully than get rid and lose the opportunity,' was his private policy.

'Any questions?' Crinklebottom asked, knowing full well there wouldn't be.

'Good,' he answered himself, 'have a pleasant day. See you tomorrow.'

And with that, he marched down through the centre and

out of the hall doorway.

The murmurs of sound rose and people began filing out of the hall, sensibly. Not at all like the rabble it would've been at my school, Billy thought to himself.

He turned around to the others and gave a little nod, as if he was onto something.

THIRTY-SEVEN

The five of them sat on a grassy bank close to the assembly hall. Poppy was picking daisies and threading them through one another, Freddie was staring at the sky. Gracie and Max were sat, almost facing away from each other and Billy was stood in front of them, like he was in charge.

'As soon as he said twenty-four cameras and seven infra-thingerme-doodahs, I knew that it was to do with wallshaveears247. I just can't work out what.'

Billy suddenly realised he was the last one standing and felt embarrassed by taking centre stage the way he had. He leaned forward to lose some height and as he did so, lost his footing and landed on his knees.

'You know, I think he's probably right,' said Gracie.

'I feel like my brain's about to explode,' Max added.

'Come on guys, we're nearly there,' Poppy said.

Freddie had been staring at the sky the whole time.

'I think Billy's right,' he said. 'Inside Watson's office there is a wall of television screens for each individual camera. We need to get in there, tonight.'

'How are we going to get in there?' moaned Poppy. 'He's always in there, even with your invisibility, you'll be seen.'

'I've got an idea,' Freddie replied, 'but we'll need Watson's phone.'

A plan was hatched. At Sunday lunch, when Watson was doing his usual breaking up of the sacred packaging, Freddie would sneak into Watson's office and take his mobile and his walkie-talkie. This was essential for the night time plan working.

They tried to go about their day as normal. Freddie and Billy tried a little table tennis. Sport, in general, was not Billy's favourite pastime but he enjoyed his short spat with the table tennis bat.

Gracie and Poppy found a quiet spot and used Poppy's device to speak to the Prime Minister.

Lunch was Sunday dinner at its best. Imagine eating Christmas Dinner at the poshest hotel in the world, that is what Billy's plate looked like. All the trimmings surrounded a nut roast with thick gravy, roast potatoes and bread and butter pudding for desert...if that sounded like MasterChef analysis, it certainly tasted like it too.

Halfway through his forkful of roast potato, Freddie stood from the table and wandered towards the doorway.

'Where are you off to young man?' came the shrill shriek of the Berry.

'Just off to the toilet, Miss.'

'Ah, yes, you'll find that through the other door.'

A little annoyed, Freddie moved over to the other door, realising he would now have to slip out of the main door and go around the building to get to Watson's office.

Less than ten minutes later, Freddie returned with his pockets bulging with two devices. You could even see the walkie-talkie protruding over his belt.

Freddie sat back down at the table and tucked into his

roast dinner.

'You were a while dear,' Mrs Berry said as she squeezed around the side of the table.

'Yes,' Freddie replied, whispering 'it was a poo not a wee.'

Mrs Berry's cheeks turned as dark as a blackberry and she shuffled off, embarrassed and muttering, 'How disgusting.'

Freddie looked across the table at the others and explained the rest of his plan.

THIRTY-EIGHT

As with all things in life, when you have found the answer to something - time flashes before you incredibly quickly. When you are stuck, like on a difficult maths question on a Friday afternoon - time drags on like you are walking through a hot desert in desperate search of some water.

The rest of that Sunday was more 'hot desert' than 'quick flash,' none of the five superheroes knew how this final piece of the puzzle was going to fit into place.

Tomorrow was their final opportunity. They all knew they had to solve the final bit and get back to the PM, so that the government could hold a press conference before Crinklebumfeatures.

There was a lot of sitting and staring into space from all five of them, trying to unlock the clues.

They had opted for 4:00am on Monday morning. And this time, it would just be Billy and Freddie, to minimise the chances of getting caught. Freddie insisted that no strength was needed, so Max would stay in bed. He was pretty sure they would not need to see through anything, so Gracie could too. If there was something language related, Poppy would be able to decipher it later. Freddie was going to use a digital camera that he had invisibly stolen from one of the photography rooms to take any photos for the group to look at and solve the riddle throughout Monday.

But what was the riddle? What was the plan?

Why me? Billy thought to himself, with every stomach eel imaginable slithering through bits of undigested roast potato and nut roast as he lay staring at his new friend, the spider, dancing on the ceiling. He really did not want to get caught by eye-mask-boy again this evening, so just before 'lights out' he subtly placed a t-shirt between the dormitory door and its frame. He had already worked out that it did not have any of the usual squeaks and pops when it opened and closed. The main purpose of the t-shirt being there, was so that the door did not make a sound.

The spider had built two additional webs now and had invited a few of his mates around to share his fly, which was clearly on its last legs and very definitely, dead.

Which one of us is the fly and which is the spider? Billy lay thinking to himself, comparing himself to Crinklebum.

When 4:30am came, Billy slid out of bed and rested his feet on the floor, in a half-crab position. He thought if he transferred his weight after his feet were planted, there was less chance of the floor creaking. He then knelt down and crawled towards the doorway on his hands and knees. This mission would be entirely pyjama-based - Freddie and he had already agreed the previous evening. Crawling towards the doorway, he noticed that nobody had moved his t-shirt and he punched the air softly as a small victory. There was just enough space to slide his fingers behind the door and prize it open gently — no squeak so far — and he managed to crawl to freedom. He left the t-shirt in the door frame for his return.

In the grand hallway everything echoed. Apart from the

matron who was on duty to care for people if they felt ill during the night, the entire school was asleep by 4:00am. That is when the last teacher walked the corridors, presumably to check that nobody was having a midnight feast or a secret party.

Why would anyone want to have a party or feast with these weirdos, Billy had thought to himself over the last few days. As he reached the bottom of the staircase, he stood and waited for Freddie.

Timing was crucial for them to be able to do this successfully.

When Freddie arrived, neither of them spoke. Just a sort of half-smile to initiate the start of it all. They would stick to the plan.

When they approached the doorway, as usual, Watson lay sprawled on his chair, his arm hanging down, this time with a half-eaten chocolate biscuit in his hand. The chocolate had melted like spread over his fingers and crumbs had fallen into a small pile on the floor.

Freddie's dressing gown pockets were bulging with a mobile phone, not the sort you could get apps on, in his left and the long aerial of a walkie-talkie poking from his right.

'Why do you need those?' Billy mouthed to him in a sticky whisper.

'I don't,' Freddie replied, 'I just didn't want to leave them up there unattended.'

Freddie gave Billy the thumbs up and he walked over to the 'danger of death - keep out' cupboard. He slid the metal latch across, noticing that two more bolts had been added since the previous day's mission.

What's the point of putting more bolts on without a padlock? Billy thought to himself.

He stepped inside, cautiously and stared up at the electrical fuse box on the wall. As you would expect for any large institution, there were hundreds of switches and to be fair, they were all clearly labelled.

Billy located 'hall lights,' 'caretaker' and 'security cameras' and placed three of his fingers over the switches. They were spread out in various places, so Billy had to reach out and stretch his arms. He looked through the doorway and gave the agreed nod. Freddie disappeared from view and Billy counted from one to ten.

He flipped all three switches at the same time and dashed through the doorway immediately. He shut the door and slid one of the bolts, running towards the plant at the end of the corridor and hiding next to Freddie.

Freddie tapped him on the shoulder in a 'well done mate' sort of way and the two of them waited. The timing had to be so perfect. Eventually, Watson appeared in the hallway brandishing the brightest torch you have ever seen. The entire corridor was in darkness, with the exception of the small skylight pouring in a pool of daylight into the floor.

Watson shone his torch around the corridor and walked like a tired zombie over to the cupboard.

'Three,' whispered Freddie.

Watson unbolted the only latch that Billy had refastened and opened the door slowly, shining his torch inside.

'Two,' added Freddie.

He stepped inside the cupboard and he took three steps forward so he was staring at the fuse box.

'One, NOW' Freddie shout-whispered.

The two of them bolted from behind the plant. Billy stopped at the doorway and closed it instantly, fastening all three latches as fast as he could. Watson instantly shone his torch at the gaps in the door and Billy moved out of the way as fast as he possibly could.

Watson fell into the trap and instantly restored the power, not realising this was not just a silly prank, it was a mission. Watson yelled in all the usual ways you would expect from a man trapped into a cupboard, frantically shaking at the door to break the latches.

Bet you regret putting another two on now, Billy thought to himself as he moved away from the door.

When Billy entered Watson's office, Freddie was stood in front of the vast array of mini television screens representing each security camera, and was taking as many photos as he could.

'Seen anything?' Billy whispered.

'Not yet, all gone to plan?' Freddie said.

'Sort of, I'm the most scared I've ever been. I've just locked a teacher in a cupboard.'

The two of them started giggling before Freddie put his finger over his lips. He snapped away at the television screens for another thirty seconds, before turning the power of the camera off and removing the memory card.

'Right, well it's lost on me, but we'll give it a go,' Freddie said. 'Remember Billy, wait until it's quiet and he's moved away from the door and then just run as fast as you can. I'll go to the art room and get these printed before pandemonium sets in. Ready?'

'Ready,' Billy replied, still gulping back down the roast potato and cauliflower cheese that the eels were playing tennis with in his guts.

Freddie disappeared and Billy was completely alone in Watson's office. The cries and shouts had softened now and as Freddie had thought, he had moved away from the doorway and plonked himself down against the wall.

Billy took a deep breath and dashed to the electrical cupboard door, unbolting all three latches in less than a second and then sprinting to the hall doorway. As he opened it and was dashing out, he felt the distinct brightness of Watson's torchlight around his feet and he disappeared back up the staircase, crawling back into his dormitory and back into bed.

He had never felt so out of breath in his life. Trying to catch your breath in silence is a very difficult thing to do, but as luck would have it - even the dancing spider on the ceiling was unmoved.

THIRTY-NINE

Billy was the last one down to breakfast, as he sat at the table, his plate piled high with toast and fruit, he still felt exhausted.

Max, Poppy and Gracie looked suitably refreshed after their night's sleep and chewing a large mouthful of cereal, Max said 'how did it go then?'

'Yes,' Freddie said 'but I was staring at them for the rest of this morning and I can't see anything.'

'How many pictures are there?' Gracie asked.

'Thirty,' Freddie said. 'That's six each, let's split them and see what we can come up with in lessons today.'

As you would have guessed, Monday morning assembly was completely overtaken by Crinklebum's ramblings over Watson being locked in a cupboard. Clearly, something similar had happened a few years previously - which was excellent for the superheroes as it decreased the probability that it could have been them, even though each of them had their suspicions that Crinkle would expect it to be them.

The five of them sat in lessons. Most of the day was spent studying their photographs in secret, as often as they could.

Billy peered at each of his, which were all photographs of a blank television screen and nothing but a strip of white electrical tape with a series of numbers on it. Although the photographs were different, they just all looked identical to Billy.

He thought back to a time when Dad had taken him to an art gallery and spent what seemed like hours looking at each painting and the accompanying caption. When a very bored Billy finally managed to persuade Dad to take him to the canteen, the flapjack and hot chocolate restored his energy enough to ask his Dad 'Why do you spend so long looking at pictures of shapes inside a black box?'

'You've got to think outside the box, Billy, somebody spent hours on that. Every picture means something, whether it's a photograph or a painting. It's somebody's thoughts, or in the case of a photograph - a memory of someone, somewhere.'

Think outside the box, Billy thought to himself over and over for the entire afternoon. But as it turned out, there just were not enough boxes to think outside of and by dinner, he had completely run out of options.

A very moody Watson was going through his regular procedure of destroying the packaging and placing it in the trough. With each hit, he seemed to be imagining he was hammering something that he really hated. Probably the little urchin who locked him in a cupboard, Billy thought to himself with a smile.

During their free time that evening, the five of them sat thinking again on the same green bank they had the previous day. Unlike other groups of young people their age, they had mastered the art of sitting in silence and being quite comfortable in one another's quiet company.

'It's just a load of blank screens and a few numbers,' Gracie said.

They all knew that, nobody was going to answer or say

anything. After a long time, Poppy sat bolt upright.

'How are the numbers presented?' she asked.

'Just a load of numbers with some full stops in between,' Max said, 'it's completely useless, I think we need to phone the PM and tell him we can't do it.'

'Hang on,' Poppy said. 'Billy, pick one of your photos and read the numbers out.'

Billy did this, although he felt it was completely pointless. Poppy thought for a long time, she was nodding her head in the way that people do when they're trying to work something out and then she started smiling.

'I've got it,' she said, 'we've done it guys.'

The four others looked to her for the golden nugget of knowledge that they had all been missing.

'It's a code. The number one represents the letter a. Right the way through to 26, which I think will be z. That's why there are dots between the numbers. Walls have ears just references the security camera televisions. The numbers must be the way that the biofuel and packaging are created.'

There was a mad scrabble from all of them from the photographs and they began studying. Gracie took a few pens from her pocket and started passing them around.

An hour or so later they all had photographs with the corresponding bits of code littered all over them. The light was fading, but there was just enough for Freddie to look at the timecode from the printouts and put them in order. The twenty-four photographs gave the correct instructions to bind the ingredients together and create the packaging and fuel.

The five of them laid back in celebration and stared up at the sky. The stars spread beautifully across the nearly-night sky and glinted and twinkled in all the right places to make it look perfect.

Billy turned his head to the side and saw tears rolling down Gracie's face.

'Are you okay Gracie?' he said softly.

'Yes,' she replied, 'it's happy tears. Just can't believe we've done it.'

The last five days were scarcely believable. When the light had finally gone, Freddie collected all the papers together and put them in the right order. Then he folded the A4 photographs and stuffed them inside his shirt.

'Shall we phone the PM?' Max said.

'Let's wait until the morning, we can't go anywhere until tomorrow night, they'd send a search party out,' Gracie said.

'You should be inside,' said a lady walking past them, 'they'll be out looking for you shortly.'

They did not see who it was at first, but they recognised Mrs Browning's voice. She was walking a scruffy little dog, holding its lead and turned briefly, giving all five of them a beaming smile and then disappearing off into the dusk.

FORTY

Billy had a strange feeling that evening, lying and staring at the spiders dancing on the ceiling. He did not often feel emotional. When his Grandma died, he remembered feeling sad and down. He walked downstairs the day after she had passed away peacefully in her sleep and found his Mum and Dad, hugging each other and crying in the kitchen.

He did not choose to go to her funeral as the thought of loads of other family being sad and crying, made him feel uneasy and weird.

His Mum had grabbed him by the hand in the kitchen and said, 'It's normal to cry Billy. Don't worry, we're alright. We just miss her, that's all.'

He had a lump in his throat, but he did not know how to cry about it. He loved his Grandma so much, she used to give him chocolate biscuits and blackcurrant juice. She always used to pour the water in before the juice and then stir it with a teaspoon afterwards, which Billy found so weird. But even the thoughts of the biscuits and the juice and the fact that he would never see her again, did not make him cry.

Maybe I just can't cry when I'm sad, he thought to himself. Maybe I can't cry anymore at all.

As he lay in his bed, staring at the spider family - which had now grown to six, tears did fill his eyes. He had never felt sorry for himself before, through all of the appointments in his life with consultants, the fitting of his hearing aid, taking the odd day off school to go to hospital – he had taken it all in his stride and not been upset about it at all.

Then he thought of Max, Gracie and Poppy, who had all gone through the same in different ways. His new friends.

Then, after one blink, the tear fell. Then another. He wiped it away with his pyjama sleeve. Here were just five normal young people all with different journeys and stories. With a little help from a weird test at school and the Prime Minister, they had all been forced together by circumstance and had become friends. Whilst he would never feel at home at Finian's, there was something homely about being with them.

He did not love the fact that his ear was a little different, he did not love the fact he had microtia...but he was starting to love himself and that was enough for the tears to keep falling until eventually, he fell asleep.

FORTY-ONE

'They're sending a helicopter for us. All we have to do is get out of the school grounds and it will pick us up at 9 o'clock,' Gracie said.

'Yes!' Max celebrated. 'I was hoping we'd get to go in one of them.'

'The PM said to leave everything where it is, all of the clothes, uniforms...just leave them in our dormitories. All we need is ourselves and our devices,' Gracie added.

'9 is a tricky time,' Poppy remarked, 'it's before lights out.'

'Yeah and we can't muck it up now,' Freddie said.

'We won't,' interrupted Billy, 'they're far too busy with Wednesday's press conference, teachers have been in meetings all morning, there's no one about.'

'Still,' Gracie answered. 'Let's be careful.'

Mrs Berry wasn't there this morning, the prefects on duty asked everybody to take their own disposable plates over to Mr Watson, who was breaking them up in the usual way.

When Billy reached his turn in the queue, there was a sudden grab to his arm and as he looked down, he saw the chocolate-biscuit-stained hand of Watson around his blazer.

'I've got very good at guessing people's future jobs' he

said in a very sinister voice, 'I think, you'd make a very good electrician Billy.'

Billy gave a half smile and nodded. 'Thanks sir. I'll think about it.'

'Nobody locks me in a cupboard and gets away with it, when I find out who it was, they'll be out of this school.'

'Absolutely, Sir. I agree.'

Then Watsit tapped him on the arm and barked 'On your way then, lad!'

Billy turned and made for the door, wiping away the handprint of Watson as he did. The entire school day was unbearably slow. Lesson after lesson of pretending to pay attention, all five of them armed with all of the knowledge that was going to bring the entire school plan to nothing. It was the oddest feeling being so powerful, yet still pretending to be hard working pupils who were good listeners.

Billy would find himself staring out of the window, admiring the freedom of the birds tweeting, flying and pooing all over the trees and grass. That'll be me soon, he thought to himself, but I won't poo on the grass.

Even dinner was excruciating. The five superheroes sat and said very little to one another. Billy did not feel hungry at all, this final slice of Finian's was the most important, escaping without being caught. Rather than eels, they were lighter butterflies today, swooping around in every direction. It was not uncomfortable, but it did stop him from eating his apple pie - which is something he had not ever imagined doing before.

It was 8:30pm, Billy was sat on his bed, pretending to read a book that they had been given in English, which was hypnotically awful. So many long words and phrases, but he was not focusing on that. He heard that same rumble as when he had first arrived.

Helicopter, Billy thought to himself. It sounded much further away this time. He imagined himself sat comfortably in the PM's office, this final ordeal being over.

He stood up. Eye-Patch, did not yet have his eye patch on and was also reading.

'Not again,' Eye-Patch said, 'where are you off to this time?'

'Just the toilet,' Billy said.

'I'm warning you, if the whole dormitory is punished because you are caught out somewhere, I'll be after you. That's a promise.' Eye-Patch pointed at Billy with his long witch-like finger, then returned to his boring book.

Billy wandered to the dormitory door, thinking to himself how creepy it was that boarding schools still referred to it as 'homework?'

It should be called dormwork, he thought to himself.

He opened the door and walked out into the corridor. Just because he never would get the chance again, he sat on the long wooden bannister and slid the entire length of it, picking up speed and falling forwards onto the floor when he reached the bottom. He fell to the ground and rolled several times, like a sausage along the floor.

He saw Watson appear out of his doorway down the next corridor, he had clearly seen Billy on the security camera. Billy darted out of the doorway and up to the same grassy bank, where the others were nowhere to be seen.

Billy's eyes wandered everywhere on the search for the others. The unmistakable face of Freddie was staring at him through the gap in the outside bin. To be clear, he was not inside the bin, but hiding behind the back of it - staring through the middle. As Billy caught his gaze, Freddie pointed across to the other side of the grassy mound. He turned his head and spotted Gracie and Poppy stood behind a large group of lockers that were positioned outside the sports hall under cover. Poppy pointed back at the doorway and Billy turned his head to see Max running out of the doorway.

As he approached Billy, he shouted 'Let's get out of here.'

Billy joined him in the run towards the end of the field. A quick glance behind them saw Poppy, Gracie and Freddie tagging behind.

'That's them, get them!' came the bellowing voice of a prefect, with a group of around six boys and girls who all began running towards the group. Billy changed course from heading towards the main entrance to back towards the foxglove field.

As Billy began running through it, he started treading down a messy path of foxgloves and the others did their best to follow suit running along the same path.

A long line of prefects stood at the base of the foxglove field, not wanting to break the rules and formed a line to blockade the superheroes in. At the end of the field, completely out of breath, the five stopped by a large oak tree.

'What now?' Gracie gasped. 'That fence behind the tree is twelve feet tall at least. We'll never get over it.'

'I've got an idea,' Freddie said. 'Wait there.'

As the four of them stood, still catching their breath, apart from the gasping for air, there was complete silence. Each of them tried to invent ways to outsmart 16 year old prefects, still stood in a strong line, with their arms folded defiantly.

Without warning, the trousers of one prefect fell to his ankles, revealing his purple spotty pants. Out of shock, the otherwise perfect prefect stumbled backwards and fell to the floor. As his next-door neighbour looked on totally bemused, his tie seemed to double in length, as if it had been pulled sharply towards the ground. She fell forward, chin first, breaking her fall with her hands at the last moment. Third in line couldn't help but laugh at his two colleagues and as he stepped to the side, he became aware that his shoe laces had been unlaced and retied together, causing he too, to lose his balance. The fourth started running in fear and looked like an invisible monster had grabbed his foot and he fell to the floor. The fifth and sixth had already began running back towards the main building in total fear.

With a series of bunny hops, trips and staggers, the other four followed suit - terrified for their lives. As the four watched on in hysterics, Freddie reappeared from back behind the sports hall with his arms in the air.

'YES Freddie,' Max shouted, with his usual fist pump that the group had learnt to love over the last few days. The four ran back down the foxglove field with as much vigour as they had done previously. When they got to Freddie, there were hugs and pats on the back through the continued breathlessness of the other four.

'You're. A. Genius, Freddie,' Billy said, through gasps of air, like he was continuously dunking his head in a bowl full of apples at Halloween.

'Let's get out of here, properly this time,' Freddie said.

They started jogging, a little slower this time, back towards the main entrance. As they did, the main gate, at least twenty feet high and made of solid wood and metal began to close. Three very large bolts began to automatically lock. As the heroes approached, Watson appeared in front of the gate, brandishing a broom.

'That's it, I told him. I said, 'Headmaster, it's definitely those five.' Nobody listens to me, nobody ever does. I knew it was you and you won't get away with this.'

'What now?' Max said.

Gracie studied Mr Watson's top pocket intently. A huge smile spread across her face.

'Billy,' Gracie said, 'go to that metal panel and punch in 010287.'

Billy did as he was told and punched the numbers in. The automatic bolts began to unlock and very slowly the doors opened.

'No!' Watson bellowed and rushed over to the small glass control room, turning a key and playing with a load of dials on a dashboard. At that same moment, in the corner of his eye, Billy saw Mrs Browning appear, with her same scruffy dog. She pulled the door of the control room, held the handle and produced a small key from her jacket pocket which she promptly locked the door with.

She winked across at the superheroes and put her thumb up, then she wandered off with her dog into the distance and without turning back said 'good luck to you.'

Watson banged on the glass and tried to open the handle and took a large set of keys from his pocket to try and locate the right one. The doors were open enough for the gates to have opened a little, certainly enough for the five of them to escape.

Dusk was definitely settling, and night was drawing in. It was certainly more light than it was dark. Unmistakable lights came down the country lane, it was clearly headlights to a vehicle. That vehicle was a jet-black jaguar with the registration plate 'CR14 KLE' and the unmistakable face of Crinklebum in the driver's seat.

'Oh... give us a break!' Poppy screamed at the top of her

lungs.

Crinklebottom had an evil smile on his face and moved his vehicle so it stood still right in front of the superheroes.

Max grabbed another small plastic container from his pocket and bit the top of it, downing it in one gulp as he has done before. He raised his left arm in the air and then placed his hand on the bonnet. With a huge scream he pushed the car backwards and into a ditch. The back wheels spent a few moments deciding whether they were going to fall into the ditch or not, but Crinkle confirmed that when he tried to open his door and the car lost its balance, ending up at a 45 degree angle in the air.

'Right. Come on,' Max said 'that's enough, let's go home.'

They ran to the field and onto the helicopter. A government official had a huge smile on his face and welcomed them with a high-five, you know how adults do when they think they are 'down with the kids.'

After placing their headsets on, the helicopter lifted off the ground. The five were still catching their breath as they saw the foxglove field, the school hall and the dormitory windows get smaller and smaller. All five superheroes just could not stop smiling. The unmistakable spot of Mrs Elsie Browning in the garden of her cottage, waving at them, was the last thing they saw before the helicopter stopped lifting and moved forward into the night sky.

FORTY-TWO

The PM stared across the table at the very tired looking superheroes with a broad grin on his face. In front of him were the complete set of briefing notes, with all of the solved data from the five in front of him in black and white.

'Well, it seems our coup paid off. What can I say, you've all been brilliant. You risked your sanity and you've given the government information that is worth billions to our economy. I propose that each and every one of you are paraded at the press conference tomorrow and I personally will have the opportunity to thank you all publicly. They're putting together the final measures for our own press conference tomorrow, so I'm just going to check up on that. We've bought you some decent takeaway pizza, so tuck into that and I'll be back in a jiffy.'

With that, the Prime Minister left the table and the room.

The five of them sat in silence. The smiles, elation and happiness had turned to nervousness and worry. Unusually, Billy was the first to speak.

'I think what we've done is brilliant.'

'Yeah, it is,' Poppy said.

'But,' Billy added, 'I really don't want to go on TV and

have all that stuff.'

'I agree,' said Gracie.

In fact, they were all in agreement. None wanted praise for what they'd done, this wasn't just a charity run being celebrated in a school assembly, this was the entire world's media that could be at their doorstep forever, asking questions that they weren't able to answer. None of them wanted fame or fortune, they just wanted to be…normal.

Max was the brave spokesperson who said all of this to the PM, who was extremely supportive.

'So, what would you like to do?' the PM asked.

'Erm…we'd like to go home,' said Gracie.

The PM nodded enthusiastically. 'Okay,' he said. 'We can arrange that for you, are you sure I can't persuade you to stay for the press conference?'

The five looked around at each other for joint reassurance.

'No thank you,' said Gracie, 'just a lift home if we could.'

'Of course,' the Prime Minister said, adding, 'in that case – we'll be in touch, as I'm sure they'll be more work for you all if you'd be willing to accept. In fact…' the Prime Minister stopped himself and smiled again at each of them. 'Don't worry about that for now,' he added 'on behalf of the entire country, I'd like to thank you all so much for all you've done.'

He rose from the table once more and gathered his papers together.

'You'll want to thank your sister too,' said Poppy.

'Yes, Mrs Browning, very helpful with everything' smiled Freddie.

The Prime Minister paused and his smile turned to a frown.

'I don't have a sister, I did have, but sadly she passed on when we were children.'

The superheroes looked at one another, aghast.

'Who was Mrs Elsie Browning, then?' asked Billy.

The Prime Minister turned to the doorway, where one of his senior advisors was flipping through a big, thick file with 'St Finian's' scribbled onto the spine. She looked over at the superheroes and then brought the folder over to the table, turned it around and pushed it across to them. There was a clear picture of Mrs Browning and some typed notes about her on the page.

'It would appear that Mrs Elsie Browning, is Mr Crinklebottom's sister.' said the senior advisor.

'No way,' Max said.

'You'll see from the notes that they had a falling out about ten years ago and Elsie stopped working at the school apart from matron duties and teaching general studies at the weekend. Because she sued Crinklebottom, she got to keep her cottage.'

'I say again, thank you all and I'll see you soon.' And with that, the PM stood and left the room, leaving all of them staring at the folder.

FORTY-THREE

It was so nice to see London from a posh car, without any eels or butterflies in your belly. Just a can of coke and a selection of chocolate bars, was all that accompanied Billy and 'Need-a-Shave' who was back in the driver's seat.

Mum and Dad had been told where Billy was and had received continued updates on his safety, but they did not know what he had been doing. They did not ask and Billy did not say anything. Dad got a phone call from the Prime Minister that evening, thanking him and Mum for their co-operation.

Dad got off the phone and ran into the living room with a huge smile on his face. 'I've just been on the phone to the Prime Minister,' he said jumping up and down. 'Billy, what were you doing?'

'Ah, it's so boring,' Billy replied.

Mum and Dad smiled at one another, as if they had some inkling into what he had been up to for the last few days but they did not ask him any further questions.

The sofa was as comfortable as he had remembered, and his room was still perfectly in place. Life was almost instantly normal.

Mum came and kissed him goodnight, holding a small packet.

'It's good to have you back, I picked up some batteries for your hearing aid today.'

Billy smiled at her and the normality of it all. She leant forward and kissed his forehead, 'My superhero,' she said before leaving the room.

Billy was asleep in a matter of seconds and slept more deeply than he had in his entire life. He was up at 7:00am and in the bathroom before everybody else.

The following day at school, after everyone had got over where he had been and Billy had given the various excuses, it was back to normal within ten minutes. People still messed about, the bullies-bullied, the lunch tasted like a plastic bag and the toilets still stank of rotten poo. Still, you could not have wiped the smile from Billy's face with wirewool. He had forgotten how brilliant his life was, how much he loved it all really and how he had a new sense of appreciation for the 'normal' part of his existence.

At 5:59pm, he dashed down the stairs and joined Mum and Dad on the sofa where they were already watching the run up to the government briefing outside 10 Downing Street. They explained how the world was going to change, what they had discovered and then they flashed to another press conference at St Finian's, whilst detailing what Mr Crinklebottom and the institution had done.

Two police officers entered, live on TV and arrested Crinkle. He was taken and was last seen being man-handled into a police car, which was filmed driving through the same gates that Billy and the others had left less than 24 hours earlier.

'This is going to change the world,' Dad said. 'That

packaging is genius…and feeding it to animals, who knew? Well, whatever you had to do with this son, I'm so proud of you.'

He looked across at Billy who looked back and saw the embarrassing sight of Dad wiping a tear from his eye.

'Stop it Dad,' Billy said, embarrassed.

'Don't be rude Billy,' Mum interjected, quickly.

Mum produced a homemade apple pie and custard and Billy wolfed it down and even had a second helping. He stayed up an hour later and watched a wildlife programme with Mum, while Dad stood and ironed some clothes and talked most of the way through it.

When it finally was time for bed, Billy walked slowly upstairs, brushed his teeth and moved across the landing to his window. He noticed a spider on his windowsill, but unlike his new friend at Finian's this one did not yet have a mansion. He opened his window and ushered the spider out.

'Go that way, you're safer building your house out there, mate,' Billy whispered at the spider.

He clambered into bed and lay down with his hands underneath his head, staring up at the ceiling.

His mattress began vibrating and he put his left hand down the side and pulled up a charger lead, on the end of which was his device…'press to talk.'

He smiled and pressed the middle of the screen, wondering if the Prime Minister was phoning to thank him personally.

Sure enough, the face of the PM popped up onto the screen.

'Hi Bill.'

'Hi, Prime Minister.'

'Erm…right…I'm sending a car on Saturday night for you. 7pm.'

'Oh right, are we having a party?' Billy asked.

'Erm...no, not exactly,' he said. 'Something's come up and I need you five back to help me solve it.'

'To do with Finian's?'

'Not exactly, no. Not at all, in fact...this is a little more dangerous...and worrying. Can you make it?'

'Yes I'll be there.'

'Excellent, enjoy the rest of your week.'

With that, the screen on his device went blank and he put it back down the side of his bed. An eel reappeared in his belly and spat a bit of apple pie up into his throat and he quickly swallowed it back down and gave his stomach a quick punch to make it go away. But it didn't.

Thanks

2020 was a tricky year for everybody and our family was no exception. I'd like to thank Tina and Hana at Microtia UK for extending deadlines and being so amenable during a particularly difficult year for me personally.

I'd also like to thank supporters of Microtia UK who have stepped in as editors, lawyers and illustrators to make this project happen for such a worthwhile cause.

Thank you to my fiancée Rosie and my three wonderful children for their support and ears as I read aloud and re-wrote chapter after chapter. Also, my Mum Evie and my Sister Hannah, who have supported me throughout this project.

Watch out for the second book in the series, which me and the fabulous team at Microtia UK are working on together in 2021. 'MI9 - The Ends of the Earth' is everything you think it's going to be and more...

What ends of the earth would you go to, to keep everyone in the country safe? Would you step out, on the world's biggest talent show and try and stop its creator from taking over?

Would you fly to a completely different country, undercover, without your friends and family by your side?

The question is, will Billy and his friends...? Find out soon in MI9: The Ends of the Earth.

ADAM ROOD

More Thanks

Our huge thanks to the following people for supporting the creation of the book.

Illustrator: Lorraine Wilkins
Lorraine created illustrations to go with every chapter of the book. The illustrations were fitting to the content of each chapter and she gave her time and illustrations for free.

Proof Reader: Aoife Loftus
Aoife gave many hours of her time for free to proof read the book and she provided some very helpful guidance.

Our children reviewers
Before we sent the book to the publisher, the following children provided us with excellent feedback on how to improve the book and on how to make it an enjoyable read for their peers:

Riya Aude Barbier-Ramaiah
Louis Salussolia
Isaac Jones
Sasha Zlotnik
Sam Zlotnik
Sofia Di Bucci
Charlie Rycroft

PROUD TO BE ME

Microtia results in underdeveloped ear(s) and affects hearing. The Microtia UK charity supports people affected by microtia. They are funded entirely on voluntary contributions and sales from this book go to the charity. Funding supports the following areas:

1. Developing research
2. Community development
3. Education and publications

Please see their website for further information and resources
www.microtiauk.org.

microtia
UK Proud to be me

Microtia Mingle is a Facebook support group for children, adults and families affected by microtia in the UK. Please email info@microtiauk.org if you would like to get in touch about the book or about microtia.